Cookies

&

Candlelight

by Elizabeth Maddrey

Other Books by Elizabeth Maddrey

Arcadia Valley Romance – Baxter Family Bakery Series
Loaves & Wishes (in *Romance Grows in Arcadia Valley*)
Muffins & Moonbeams
Cookies & Candlelight (September 2017)
*Donuts & Daydreams (*March 2018)

The 'Operation Romance' Series
Operation Mistletoe
Operation Valentine
Operation Fireworks
Operation Back-to-School

The 'Taste of Romance' Series
A Splash of Substance
A Pinch of Promise
A Dash of Daring
A Handful of Hope
A Tidbit of Trust (Summer 2017)

The 'Grant Us Grace' Series
Joint Venture
Wisdom to Know
Courage to Change
Serenity to Accept

The 'Remnants' Series:
Faith Departed
Hope Deferred
Love Defined

Stand alone novellas
Kinsale Kisses: An Irish Romance

Non-Fiction

A Walk in the Valley: Christian encouragement for your journey through infertility

For the most recent listing of all my books, please visit my website.

For everyone who's ever taken a chance on love.

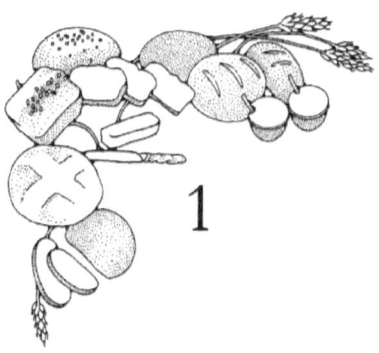

1

"Oh, thank goodness. I wasn't sure you'd actually get here in time. Bring them this way."

Micah stood rooted to the front step as the woman with fiery red hair disappeared into the house. Questions zipped through his mind, but there was no point asking them. She was gone. Hefting the two paper shopping bags full of cookies, muffins, and bread, he tentatively stepped into the foyer and followed down the hall in her wake.

That hair. Where did red like that come from? It was like liquid flame spilling down to her shoulders.

He gave himself a firm mental shake and stepped into a large, two-story living area. The two outside walls were floor to ceiling windows and sunlight spilled over the space, highlighting the gleaming mission-style furniture and brightly colored ceramic pots scattered around the room.

"In here. Look, I'm running behind. Can you put them on these platters?"

Micah spun. An enormous kitchen sprawled across the back of the room, separated from where he stood by an island with six stools lined up under the overhang.

He cleared his throat. "Ms. Johnson?"

"That's me. Serena's fine. Here are the platters, I really need to hurry. My guests are going to be here in fifteen minutes."

"We don't really..." Micah stopped and sighed. She'd disappeared again. Fine. He could throw cookies onto trays. But Malachi was getting a piece of his mind when he got back to the bakery. Not only was her place so far north of town it was practically another country, but he wasn't a caterer.

Micah lifted the bags to the counter and turned to the sink. He flipped the handle on the faucet and thrust his hands under the water. Soap. Was there...he spotted a ceramic bottle with a pump on the top. Worth a shot. A girly and floral aroma permeated the air as he scrubbed up a thick lather. Micah wrinkled his nose. Hopefully the scent of the cookies would get rid of that. The last thing he needed was to get back to the bakery smelling like a summer meadow. His brothers would never let him hear the end of it.

Hands clean, he pulled the boxes of cookies and muffins from the larger bags and made a circle of muffins in the center surrounded with cookies. If the woman—Serena—wanted them separated, she should've stuck around. Or done it herself. Delivery didn't mean set up.

She clipped back into the room on mile high heels. "That looks great. Thanks. Ever made cucumber sandwiches?"

"Do I look like an eighty year-old British woman?" He heard the testiness in his voice but honestly, he'd fulfilled his duties when he brought her the order. He had work he should be getting back to. And fine, there weren't many customers on a Saturday, but he'd just started reading a new space opera.

Serena's grin flashed and her gaze flicked from his head to his toes. Something glinted in her eyes. Appreciation? Couldn't be. Women didn't ogle that obviously. Did they?

"Not really. Then again, cucumber sandwiches aren't that limited in audience." She checked the slim gold watch on her wrist. "Look. I could use a hand. All you have to do is spread cream cheese. Okay?"

Micah lifted a shoulder. "Why not?"

"That's the spirit." She smacked a kiss to his cheek, pointed to a long, oval platter, and gestured vaguely toward the fridge before floating out of the room. "Be right back. Stuff's in the fridge."

Micah shook his head. He ought to leave. Just walk back out the front door, get in his car, and head back to the book that was waiting for him by the cash register. Except...he could hear Jonah's chiding voice in his head. A big order like this one—without even a flinch at the extra charge they'd added for last-minute prep and delivery? Serena Johnson was the kind of customer they needed to keep happy so she'd think of them again when she had...whatever kind of party this was.

A well-stocked knife block sat beside the stove. Micah slid each knife out, one by one, until he found something serrated. It wasn't technically a bread knife, but it looked like it would fit the bill. Cucumber sandwiches. His Nana had been big on tea parties with his big sister, Ruth, and interested or not, he and his brothers had been forced to endure more of them than was strictly necessary. Particularly when they'd all rather have been swinging from the ropes Pops had tied high in the branches of their backyard trees. At least the torture was paying off now.

Micah cut thin slices of bread. Not quite transparent, but certainly daintier than any slice he normally prepared. A quick trip to the fridge revealed the cream cheese and a container of sliced cucumbers. At least she hadn't been wrong about being able to find the ingredients. With another sigh, he began the process of assembling sandwiches.

Serena breezed back into the room, the same floral scent as the soap seemed to hover around her. "I really appreciate this." She frowned. "I didn't catch your name."

He snorted. "There wasn't time for introductions, apparently."

She grinned. "Kiln openings always make me nuts. It's why I only do maybe two a year. Couldn't get out of this one, though. And I still don't know your name."

He set the knife down on the lip of the cream cheese container and held out his hand. "Micah Baxter. It's a pleasure to meet you."

She clasped his hand and laughed. "No, it isn't. I've driven you crazy. But I appreciate you being a good sport. I don't suppose..."

Whatever she would have said was cut off by the doorbell. She rolled her eyes and strode down the hallway.

Whatever. Micah rubbed his hand on his jeans, trying to erase the tingles. The air in here had to be dry. What other reason could there be for that little frisson of electricity when she shook his hand?

Laughter echoed from the entryway to the kitchen. Micah shoved down his curiosity, washed his hands a second time, and focused on the sandwiches. She hadn't said if they should be open-faced or closed. So he'd make some of each. And if guests were already arriving, why hadn't she planned ahead better? Not that he could have gotten there all that much sooner than he had with a last-minute order this large.

Micah began arranging the sandwiches on a platter. The patterns on the thing were interesting—as if fern leaves had been dipped in ink and pressed to the plate. He ran his finger over the design. Definitely unique. And the bold teal accents were almost too nice to cover with food. Although that would give people the pleasure of revealing it when they took something to eat. Maybe that was part of her plan.

A kiln opening. Did that mean she'd made these? If so, the woman had talent.

Footsteps announced Serena's return with her guests in tow. "Oh. Open-faced. What a good idea. I hadn't even thought of that. Micah Baxter, I'd like you to meet my parents, Carl and Laura Johnson."

Micah brushed his hand off again before taking each of theirs in turn. "Nice to meet you."

"Have you known Serena long?" Laura cast an appraising eye over him before arching a brow at her daughter.

"About twenty minutes. My brothers and I own a bakery in town. I brought her order up."

Laura laughed.

Carl grinned. "And she roped you into helping. Sounds like my girl."

Serena shrugged. "I needed a hand. Speaking of which, could you each grab one of those and take them out to the studio? You'll see where they go once you get there. I should double-check that the signs in the driveway are clear so people don't come to the house."

"They're fine. We didn't figure you'd mind if we came here first." Carl hefted the large plate of cookies and muffins.

"Plus, we're early." Laura picked up the second, smaller plate. "Grab those sandwiches, would you, Micah?"

Serena's eyes sparkled with quiet laughter. "I'll meet you in the back in just a minute."

Well. At least he knew where Serena got it. He picked up the platter and followed after the Johnsons. Maybe after this he could make his escape.

French doors opened from the living room onto a deck that ran the entire width of the house. He followed

Serena's parents across and down a set of steps to a wide paved area in front of a smaller building made of wood and glass. Micah could hear the gurgle of Clover Creek. He'd known it was close, but Serena's property must end at the bank. The sound lightened his heart. He'd always been a sucker for flowing water.

Stepping into the studio was like entering a high-end ceramics gallery. Natural light flooded the space. Shelves and tables displayed pots of every imaginable shape and size—from something that could be used to hold pencils at a desk to a container that sat on the floor and reached the middle of his thigh. What did you use something that size for?

The designs and colors were dazzling.

"Bring that over here." Laura's voice held a smile.

Micah tore his gaze away from Serena's art and crossed the room to a long table where the platters of cookies had already been set. He put the sandwiches in the center and looked at the back half of the building.

The contrast was stark. The rug stopped on the other side of the food table, revealing a plain concrete floor. Tables were pushed against the wall, some with strange utensils stacked on them. A potter's wheel took up the center of the room, though there appeared to be a second one on the back wall. Then there were the shelves. Many were empty, but others held bowls of varying sizes. They weren't colorful, though. Were they unfinished?

"Never seen a potter's studio before?" Carl ambled over to stand beside him, his hands in his pockets. "Serena's is a little fancier than most, I think."

"Does she—what's it called?—cook them in here too?"

Carl chuckled. "She has her own kilns, but they're through that closed door on the back wall. That's a separate room with better ventilation. The clay lets off gasses when it's being fired. You don't want that spewed out into where you're working if you can help it."

Micah nodded and turned back to the more-finished area that was clearly her showroom. "Impressive."

"Thanks." Serena grinned and came to the table. She shifted everything a little before snagging a macaron and biting into it. "These are good. I appreciate your help. I know it wasn't your job. If you'd like to stay for the party, you're more than welcome."

"I...thanks. But I should get back. It was nice to meet you." Micah turned and waved at Carl and Laura. "All of you. I hope your party goes well."

Maybe one of his lamer statements. Micah stuffed his hands in his pockets and headed for the door. What else was he supposed to say? Was she hoping to sell a lot? Presumably. But he didn't want to say something about that and have it end up being, oh who knew, some kind of weird look-but-don't-buy kind of thing. Why was he even still thinking about it? He reached for the handle of his car door.

"Micah?"

He turned and his lips eased into a smile as his eyes landed on the dark-haired policewoman who was a frequent visitor at the bakery. "Gloria. What are you doing here?"

She gave a dismissive wave. "Serena and I have been friends since she moved out here. I could ask you the same."

"She needed food for whatever this is. I brought it up."

"I thought Malachi did all the deliveries?"

Micah shrugged. That was the plan, but with Ruth slammed at the bed and breakfast and her new husband, Corban, in the thick of harvest, Malachi was helping out where he could, leaving Jonah and Micah to juggle the bakery. "Jonah and I flipped a coin. I lost."

Gloria snickered. "Was it that bad?"

"Not really. Just...answer me this. Would you ask someone you've never met before to make cucumber sandwiches for you?"

Gloria's face split into a grin. "Nope. But Serena totally would. Go back to the bakery, Micah. I imagine you're desperate to get back to your book. What is it today?"

"A new epic sci-fi novel by an author I'd never heard of, but the write up sounded interesting."

"And is it?"

"Don't know. I made it through two sentences of the prologue before she called with a huge order that she should've placed last week. And a need for delivery."

"Sounds like Serena." Gloria shook her head. "But at least I know the food'll be good this time. Last one of these she did, she served sandwich cookies from the grocery store. The generic kind. See ya."

Micah frowned and watched Gloria stride toward the studio. He didn't know Serena, but he couldn't shake the idea that she and Gloria were an odd pair to be friends. Gloria embodied routine—as a police woman she probably had to. Serena, on the other hand, appeared to be about as flighty as they came.

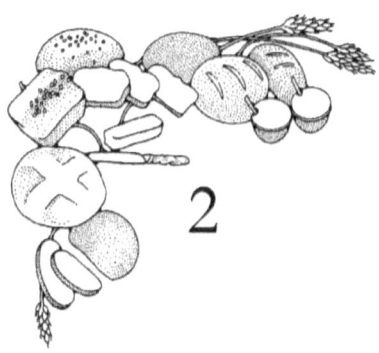

2

Serena slid her feet out of her heels and groaned. "So much better."

"I don't know why you wear those things." Gloria shook her head and stacked the empty platters on top of one another.

Serena and her mother exchanged a knowing look. "You either *get* shoes or you don't. Honestly, how are we friends?"

"I didn't give you a speeding ticket on your first day in town when you were late to your appointment to close on this house. Evidently that made you decide we were going to be friends. Haven't been able to shake you since."

Laura chuckled. "Serena's always had good taste in friends. It's nice to see you, Gloria. I'm glad you could come."

"Same goes." Gloria picked up the stacked platters. "I'm glad the opening went well."

Serena nodded and grabbed her shoes and cell phone. "It really did. I sold a little over half the pieces I had out and got some custom orders. It was worth doing with the Dieberts and Masons both close enough to make it. They're such good online customers, it was wonderful to meet them in person. The handful of others was just a bonus."

"Hear that, Laura? We're a bonus." Carl shook his head. "It's not like we flew out here from California for this or anything."

"Oh, Dad, you know what I meant." She leaned over and kissed his cheek. "Come on, let's go back in the house and sit down. You can tell me all about what's going on in L.A."

Gloria pressed the platters into Serena's arms. "I've gotta run. I traded shifts so I could make this, and I need to get in and start on some paperwork. I was right about using A Slice of Heaven though, wasn't I?"

"You were. I guess I'll see about their weekly deliveries. Fresh bread is always nice." Serena pressed her lips together. Seeing Micah again, on a weekly basis, wouldn't hurt any either. Not that she was looking for anything to develop between them. But there was no law against admiring God's creation.

"Or come into town and pick it up. Stop by and see your local police officer. Grab some coffee. Stop living like a hermit." Gloria checked her watch again and waved before dashing out the door.

Serena frowned. She didn't isolate herself. She was just busy.

"Are you being a hermit, dear? That's unlike you." Laura patted Serena's cheek before scooping up an armful of dishes to carry back to the house.

"You can leave those, Mom, I'll get them later." Serena sighed when her mother continued collecting mugs. It was so like her. Her dad just shrugged and grabbed what her mom missed. "Or not. Thanks."

She followed her parents across the driveway to her house, pausing for a moment to admire the glass and wood that made up most of the structure. Who would have imagined finding a house like this nestled near a river in Idaho? She would've gone wherever the house was. She hadn't had a particular urge toward any location beyond getting away from L.A. Only bittersweet memories had pointed her in this direction to start her search. Her stomach knotted and she battled back the recollections. There was no point in opening that door. The past was the past.

When the dishes were in the dishwasher or resting in the sink waiting for the next load, Serena curled up in an oversized chair while her parents cuddled together on the couch.

"So what's all the latest?"

Her mom smiled. "We're having a party for the Fourth of July. Can you come out? Your father's convinced some of his costars to come, and I suspect most of the gang from my latest will as well. There are some big names."

Serena shook her head. Her dad had held a steady job on a popular daytime soap since before she was born. His costars were like family. A dysfunctional one, most of the time. But still family. Her mother said she was semi-retired, though she still managed to make a movie every eighteen months. "When did you wrap? I thought you had several weeks left?"

"Oh, you know how it goes. There are still some bits and pieces to do, but we're close enough to having it all taken care of that I could slip away for the weekend."

"And it gave me a chance to test the little plane I've been thinking of buying." Her dad leaned forward and plucked a wide, shallow bowl from the middle of the coffee table. "When did you make this?"

"A couple of weeks ago. I liked it too much to put it out with everything this afternoon. I'll have to list it online, I know. But I want to enjoy it for a while. You're serious about flying? I thought the lessons were just for fun." Serena laced her fingers together as the tension in her stomach spread into her muscles. So much could go wrong in a little plane. People died in accidents all the time. Without thinking, she ran her fingers along the old scar that slashed along her jaw line from one ear to the corner of her mouth. Or they lived through them.

And sometimes that was worse.

"You know your father. Once he gets an idea in his head." Her mother gave an elegant shrug. "So will you come? We could fly out and pick you up. Everyone misses you."

Serena shook her head. "I don't think so, but I appreciate the invite. Send me pictures. And give everyone my love."

Her dad frowned. "Serena...are you sure? Is this really what you want? It's been five years."

Five years. It could be a hundred years and she didn't think she'd be any closer to being ready to go back.

"That's a long time—almost a lifetime—in the business." Her mother's smile was tight. "You're risking your future."

She sighed. Her parents meant well. Hollywood was all they knew. They'd both grown up in the movie industry. Her grandparents had been actors and then directors. There'd never been any question that her parents would continue the family business. Nor had there been an option for Serena. She'd loved it for many years. But that had ended five years—a lifetime—ago.

"I'm happy here. This is my future now. I don't expect you to understand, just to respect my choice."

"We do. You have to know that. We just miss you." Her mother reached across to squeeze Serena's hand. "And you had such a bright, promising career ahead of you."

"I think I still do." Serena smiled and flipped her hand over so she could return her mother's squeeze. "I'm grateful you care."

When her parents had left and the sun was beginning to sink in the sky, Serena carried a mug of tea out onto the deck. The summer evening was warm and full of insect noises. She leaned on the rail and looked out through the trees to the glimpse of river at the back border of her property. God had brought her here to Arcadia Valley. She'd never been able to explain that to her parents—probably wouldn't if they continued to think she was insane for believing in Jesus in the first place. But she'd keep praying for them and maybe one day they'd be willing to listen with more than a polite smile on their faces.

Serena pulled into the post office parking lot and scowled. Why were there never any parking spaces near the door? If people weren't taking packages in to mail, why couldn't they use the spots farther away? With another frown at the full rows of spots, she pulled her SUV into a space in the back row and dragged the dolly out of the trunk. When her boxes were loaded on, she started toward the small brick building. With this many cars in the lot, she was probably in for a long wait.

"Hey, you." Gloria Sinclair stopped her police cruiser and leaned out the window. "Those the mail orders from your kiln opening Saturday?"

"Yeah. Didn't see you at church yesterday. I was going to see if you wanted to hit up lunch somewhere."

Gloria tapped the steering wheel. "Had to work. I could catch lunch today though, maybe when you're done here?"

She didn't have that much to do after she got the boxes in the mail. "Sure. That sounds good. Fire and Brimstone?"

The radio in Gloria's car squawked and she held up a finger as she cocked her head to the side. She grabbed her mic and spoke into it before turning back to Serena. "I gotta run. Text me."

Serena stepped back as the lights on Gloria's cruiser lit up and she pulled out of the parking lot going a bit faster than seemed warranted. There weren't that many big emergencies in Arcadia Valley. Or maybe there were. Serena lived outside of town. Far enough away that she probably shouldn't comment on what was or was not common.

She smiled a greeting to the middle-aged woman in front of her in line at the post office and carefully lowered the front of the dolly.

"Those are some big packages." The woman nodded to Serena's stack.

Serena nodded and reached into her purse for a business card. "I'm a potter. Most of my business is online these days, but I have events now and then. If you're interested, you can follow my blog to be up to date with anything I have going on. These are orders from a kiln opening I did on Saturday. A couple of clients didn't want to risk taking them in the car or on the plane with them. So I'm shipping them."

"Oh. How interesting." The woman took the card. "Serena's a lovely name. You know, there was an actress several years ago named Serena. But she had a fancy last name. Oh what was it? My daughters loved her—she did a TV show about aliens and some of those teenaged movies. You know the ones?"

Serena chuckled. The directors of those movies would be appalled to hear them categorized as such, but the woman wasn't wrong. "I do. Are you thinking of Serena VanderMay?"

"That's the one. She was a lovely young woman. You look a little like her, actually. Tragic, though, how she died."

"Died?" Serena gestured for the woman to scoot up in line and inched her stack of boxes closer.

"Oh, yes. It was five, maybe six years ago now. Some sort of plane crash. You know those tiny planes. And, well, Hollywood types. Probably the pilot was drunk or stoned. Still, I think she was eighteen? Just tragic."

She'd been twenty-one, and the pilot had a seizure as he was landing. There were no drugs or alcohol involved. Serena worked to school her expression.

"No use in being upset about it now. But she was a pretty young woman. You should look her up online. You really do have a striking resemblance. Oh, that's me. I'll look up your pottery online." The woman waved the business card before tucking it into her pocket on her way to the counter.

Serena took a deep breath. Then another. She was working on a third, her stomach still a tight knot that showed no signs of loosening, when the postal worker motioned her forward. Push it aside. There'd be time to think about what it meant later.

Much later.

Serena dropped her phone on the table at Fire and Brimstone and looked around the crowded pizza place. When she'd let Gloria know that she was finished at the post office, her friend had texted that she should still be able to make lunch, but that was twenty minutes ago.

The server stopped by the table again. "Need another soda?"

Serena shook her head. "I'll just go ahead and order."

"Okay. What can I get you?"

"I'll take the feta, spinach, and sun dried tomato. And I guess some water. If I drink another soda, I'll be up all night."

The server chuckled. "I'll get that right in."

Serena's phone buzzed. She swiped it and frowned at the text. Gloria wasn't going to make it after all. At least she got good pizza out of the deal, but maybe she should switch her order to carry-out. If she could catch the server's eye.

"Hey. Serena, right?"

"That's me." She looked up from her phone into the face of the cute guy from the bakery. What was his name? It was a book of the Bible, but that didn't narrow it down all that much.

"Micah Baxter. We met Saturday? I—it's crowded—I was hoping maybe I could join you?"

"Sure." She gestured to the empty spots at the table. "I thought my friend was joining me, but she just bailed. If I can get the server's attention I'm going to get my pizza to go, then you can have the whole table. You've got someone coming, right?"

He shook his head. "Just me. I needed a few minutes away from the bakery."

"So you came to a pizza shop?" Weren't the smells basically the same, at the base?

Micah laughed. "Sometimes you just need a slice. And if I don't use my break to get lunch, I end up eating muffins or whatever's sitting in the display."

"That's not a bad thing, is it? I really liked what you brought on Saturday."

He lifted a shoulder. "Try it for a couple days running."

She grinned. "Fair point."

The server stopped at the table. "What can I get you?"

"I'll do the feta, spinach, and sun dried tomato and water. Thanks."

Serena raised her eyebrows. He liked the same pie she did? "Well, you've got good taste in pizza. I'll give you that."

"Yeah? It's the first one I tried and I haven't managed to convince myself to branch out since."

"It's a favorite of mine, too. In fact, it ought to be out soon." She tilted her head to the side and considered the man across the table from her. He was handsome and, if Saturday was any indication, a good sport. Maybe he was worth getting to know. "So tell me the top three things I need to know about Micah Baxter."

He laughed. "It's like a job interview."

"Hopefully not quite as terrifying."

"Maybe a tiny bit less." He held up his thumb and index finger about a quarter inch apart. "Let's see. You don't have my résumé in front of you, so I guess I'll start with the basics. I'm twenty-nine and have three siblings, one of whom is my twin. But he's younger. It's important to remember that."

"Important to you or to him?"

"Me. Obviously. You didn't ask about him."

Serena laughed.

"It's just the four of us now. Our parents," he paused and cleared his throat, but his voice was thick when he resumed speaking, "they've been gone a little over six years now."

"I'm so sorry." What must that be like? As much as she struggled to relate to her parents, she knew they were there for her if she needed them.

"Thanks. Let's see, what else? I've been in Arcadia Valley for a little over a year and, for the most part, like it. Before that, I was in D.C. at an afterschool tutoring-slash-childcare center. I miss those kids." He frowned and looked down at his hands before shrugging and offering a grin. "And that's probably plenty."

The waitress appeared and slid Serena's pizza and two plates onto the table before disappearing again.

"Want a slice to tide you over 'til yours gets here?" A guy who worked with kids—voluntarily—and missed them when he moved away? Definitely worth getting to know. Serena squashed the twinge of pain that the mention of kids always brought. She was always on the lookout for new friends. Just because she wasn't in

Hollywood anymore didn't mean she didn't need or want people around her. And her circle here in Arcadia Valley was still fairly small—and full of shallow relationships. Most people didn't recognize her, and she didn't go out of the way to clue them in. Of her friends in Arcadia Valley, Gloria was the only one she'd told. It was nice to have everything out in the open with one friend, even if she had a job that meant she wasn't always reliable.

"You sure?"

She shrugged. "Don't see why not. It's the same, right?"

Micah pushed his plate across the table. "Then yeah, thanks. It smells so good in here that I always end up starving long before my food gets here."

Serena slid a slice of pizza onto his plate before taking one for herself. She watched him for the space of several heartbeats before asking, "Do you mind if we say grace?"

"Not at all." Micah folded his hands in his lap and held her gaze. "Did you want me to do it?"

"That'd be lovely." Serena bowed her head, a tiny smile on her lips.

Micah cleared his throat. "Dear Jesus, thank you for this food and for letting me find someone to share a table with. Bless this meal to our bodies, and our bodies to Your service. Amen."

"Amen." Serena reached for her fork and knife. As prayers went, it was nothing to write home about, but it got the job done. What had she expected? Realistically, she wouldn't have done anything different. They were, virtually, strangers sharing a table. It was enough that he was comfortable praying. "So you've been here a year, you said?"

Micah paused, the slice of pizza halfway to his mouth. "About that, yeah."

"Where do you go to church?" It was a sneaky—no, subtle—way of probing more about his spiritual life. But she couldn't quite bring herself to just ask if he'd ever made a decision to follow Jesus.

"Grace Fellowship. I keep thinking I'll try Arcadia Valley Community at some point, just to see how it is, but I like Grace. And my whole family goes there, which makes it nice." He shrugged and bit into the pizza.

"Small, though. You don't mind everyone knowing when you miss a week?" Serena cut her pizza into bite-sized pieces before spearing one.

He chuckled. "Not really. At least you know they care, right? It's a nice change from the monster church I went to in D.C. I'd be surprised if anyone has even noticed I'm not there anymore."

"No way." Admittedly, her church experiences were fairly new in the grand scheme of things, but there were small groups and ministries to plug into. "Surely someone noticed."

"Maybe one or two people. Aside from the friends I told, obviously. But I'm not what you'd call an extrovert. It's not like I'm a recluse who runs away when someone tries to talk to me, but I didn't make a point of searching out opportunities to join groups." He shrugged and angled a glance at her. "You're a joiner, aren't you?"

"Yeah, that's probably accurate." She studied his face and laughed. "I don't consider it a bad thing."

"I didn't mean it that way." Micah polished off the slice of pizza. "So. How'd you get into pottery?"

"That's a long story." Serena waited while the server dropped off Micah's pizza and their checks.

Micah transferred a slice from his pan to hers and put another on his plate. "Which, as I have a sister, I know is code for 'I don't want to talk about it.' That's fine. Tell me something you don't mind sharing."

"It's not that I mind. It really is a long story." Serena took another bite and considered. She didn't usually lead off with an in-depth retrospective of her life. And he hadn't asked, as most people did, if she knew the similarity she bore to Serena VanderMay. It was refreshing to have the chance to just be Serena Johnson from the beginning. "My grandmother threw pots—that means she made them—in her garage as a hobby. I always thought it was neat to watch."

"That's kind of how we got into bread. Although, it's really more my brother Jonah and my sister Ruth who are the driving force. I help with the baking when I'm needed and otherwise run the front counter. My twin, Malachi, handles the business end of things and does deliveries."

"Deliveries? So why were you on delivery duty Saturday?"

Micah shrugged. "Mal had a date. He's getting married in September, and I think they went into Twin Falls to do a cake tasting."

"Fun. Did they choose one?"

Micah shook his head. "He's still angling to get Jonah to do the cake. Jonah did Ruth's in January and it was amazing, so it's hard to blame him."

"So why isn't Jonah doing it?" That seemed like an easy thing for one sibling to do for another. Serena got the sense that the Baxter family was a tight-knit unit.

"Oh, I think he will. He just has to gripe about it for a little while first."

"It's June. He waits much longer your brother's fiancée is going to have panic attacks thinking about getting a cake reserved in time. Tell him he should get a move on and decide." Men clearly didn't understand how weddings happened. Even smaller ones took time and planning. For that matter, so did elopements. She steered her thoughts away from that line of thinking and looked around. Micah's pizza was completely gone. She'd managed exactly a single slice of hers, which was really where she should stop if she didn't want to balloon up two sizes. Yet another difference between men and women, unfair though it was.

"I'll mention that to him." A chime sounded from across the table. Micah tugged his phone free and tapped it. "That's my alarm. I should run. Thanks for letting me share your table."

"Anytime."

Micah stood and pulled out his wallet. He tossed some bills onto the check. "It was nice to see you again."

He was winding his way through the tables to the door before she could respond. It had been nice to see him again, too. More so than she'd anticipated. She glanced down at the money he'd left. Sneaky. He was sneaky.

Serena stacked the checks together and put his cash on top of both before raising her hand to try and catch the server's eye. She needed a box for the rest of her pizza. Since he'd ended up paying for her lunch and dinner, was she supposed to count it as two dates? Or just the one?

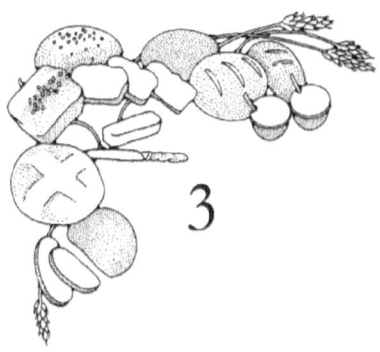

3

Micah turned as Jonah pushed through the door that separated the kitchen from the front of the bakery. "Hey."

Jonah crossed to the coffee station they'd set up for customers and reached for a mug. "Hey yourself. How's your book?"

"What book?"

"How should I know? You always have one, though."

Micah chuckled. It was true enough. He'd finished the space opera in the morning and had moved on to a fantasy he'd grabbed for free from one of the various e-book deal emails he subscribed to. "So far the story isn't living up to the cover. I'll give it another hour before I give up."

"Bummer. I know you hate that. Want coffee?" Jonah poured steaming liquid into his mug and jiggled the carafe.

"I'm good." He checked his phone. It was about time for Gloria to pop into the bakery for her daily flirting session with Jonah. Gloria was friends with Serena. Maybe she'd...no. This wasn't high school. He wasn't going to dig for details about someone by subtly interrogating her friend. Plus, he'd never been particularly good at subtle. "Mal still back there?"

"Last I checked. He was grumbling about payroll taxes earlier, so you're on your own if you interrupt him."

Micah winced. His brother was a bear when it came to taxes—they made him grumpy. And yet, watching Jonah and Gloria skate around their attraction to one another was almost painful. "You ever going to ask her out?"

Coffee sloshed over the edge of Jonah's mug as he stiffened. "I'm not looking for a relationship. I'm not good at them. You know that."

Micah made a rude noise. "I can't believe you're still letting that woman in your head."

"Yeah? You try getting her out." Jonah scowled.

"Sorry, man. I still think—"

"Just...don't, okay?" Jonah sipped from his mug and turned to look out the window that spanned the front of the bakery.

If he ever got his hands on Melissa...he didn't consider himself a violent man, but the mind tricks she'd played on Jonah pushed Micah closer than he'd thought possible. He cleared his throat. "Since you're already in a bad mood...I thought I'd give you a little nudge about Malachi's wedding cake."

Jonah turned, fixing Micah with a glare that could melt steel. "Seriously?"

Micah shrugged. "It's like three months out. They need to know."

"Fine. Go tell Mal I'll make their cake. Then ask him if he has any tips on how you can learn to mind your own business."

He fought the laugh that tried to escape. The Baxter siblings weren't particularly adept at staying out of each other's business. Jonah knew that. And that none of them would have it any other way. Still, with Jonah in a mood, vacating the premises was probably the better course of action.

Micah crossed the kitchen, breathing in the lingering scent of the chocolate chip cookies that were this week's special. Jonah had been playing with some chocolate-filled croissants as well, but hadn't been satisfied with how they turned out. Yet. He'd get it eventually. He always did. For now...Micah snagged two cookies off a cooling rack and angled toward the closet of a room Malachi used as the office.

He waved a hand where it would catch Malachi's eye and held out the cookie when his brother looked up. "Time for a break?"

"Oh yeah." Malachi grabbed the treat and bit it in half.

Micah dropped into the second chair that was shoehorned into the space. "I have some good news."

"Yeah? I could use some. What is it?" Malachi finished the cookie and brushed the crumbs off his desk, switching to sign language.

Micah smiled and switched as well. Since his brother had lost his hearing at a young age, he read lips just fine, and could speak well enough, but signing let

Micah chew without worrying about spraying cookie crumbs everywhere. "Jonah's doing your wedding cake, if you still want him."

"Really? How'd you swing that?"

That was less enthusiastic than he'd expected. Did Mal *not* want Jonah to do it? "I mentioned it was getting down to the wire and he needed to put you out of your misery. Should I not have said anything?"

Malachi ran a hand through his hair before continuing to sign. "No. It's good. Ursula will be excited. I'm just...it's taxes. I'll be happy tomorrow."

Micah grinned. "All right."

"How was lunch? Sorry I couldn't go."

"It was good. I ended up sharing a table with the woman from Saturday's delivery."

"Oh?" Malachi's eyebrows shot up.

"There's no 'oh' with that expression. You know how busy it gets in there. She was alone and had space, so I asked if I could join her."

"And she said yes."

Micah shrugged. Would someone really say no? It seemed unlikely. "We had a nice conversation. I paid, and came back."

"Did you pay for her pizza, too?"

He shifted in his seat. Malachi always saw too much—understood just a little more than was comfortable. "Yeah. So what?"

"Sneaky way to get the first date out of the way."

"Only if she decides she's open to a second. Which I haven't even decided if I'm going to ask for."

Malachi shook his head and signed, "Keep telling yourself that."

"Sometimes being a twin is a pain in the butt."

Malachi laughed. "Tell me something I don't know."

Micah thought of the electricity along his arm when he'd brushed against Serena in her kitchen. That was something his brother didn't know. And he'd do what he could to keep it that way.

"Heard you went on a date today at lunch. I need details." Ruth leaned across the counter at the bakery and snagged a cookie from the jar.

"How—what? No. I ate pizza. I don't even know how you're hearing about this." Micah crossed his arms over his chest. It had to be Malachi. The twerp.

"I have my sources. And no, it's not your brother."

Micah eyed his sister. "Ursula then?"

Red spread across Ruth's cheeks. "I'm not saying."

"You don't have to. You've always been terrible at keeping secrets." It was one of the things he loved about his sister. At least when she was supposed to keep secrets from him. He wasn't so sure about it working the other way. "It was just lunch, and an accidental meeting at that. I doubt very much Serena would classify it as a date."

"Pretty name. Who is she?"

Micah sighed. "I delivered some baked goods to her on Saturday and ran into her again this afternoon. She's a potter. Lives north of town—sort of near that farm that has all the things for kids. What's its name? Big something."

"Bigby Farm?" Ruth shook her head. "You don't pay any attention to things that don't directly impact your day-to-day life, do you?"

He shrugged. He wasn't in the market for horseback riding lessons or a day camp for kids. So why would he?

"They're great. I send a lot of my clients their way—or I try to, at least. It's pretty up there."

"Yeah. Serena has a nice setup. Her house is...cool. Modern and full of light. Her studio, too. And her pots are unique. I've never seen anything like them before. I actually thought I might talk to Jonah about buying some coffee mugs for the bakery from her. Maybe some little plates for people who want to eat in." They could probably arrange to set up a little sign saying who made them and how to get in touch with her, too. Free advertising was never a bad idea.

"Hmm. What's she look like?"

A memory of her bright copper hair floating at her shoulders, highlighting her full lips when she smiled flashed through his mind. "Pretty. She looks a lot like that actress from the show we used to tease Malachi for watching."

"Which one? There were so many." Ruth grinned. "The two of you had horrible taste in TV."

"That's because he couldn't hear how bad the acting was. Reading the subtitles doesn't give the full cheesy effect. It was the one where the alien superhero kids hid on Earth and tried to be high school students while defending us from invasions by all the myriad evil races intent on our destruction."

Ruth laughed. "Okay. I remember that one. And...if I recall, you were the one with a crush on the main actress. Mal only watched 'cause you had it on anyway."

Heat crept up Micah's neck. His sister had always had a good memory. He hunched his shoulders. "Yeah, well. She was hot."

"So, you think Serena's hot?" Ruth drummed her fingers on the counter. "When can I meet her? You should bring her to dinner on Sunday."

"Whoa. Back up. I've met her twice in the last three days. It's a *teeny* bit early for a family dinner." Micah fought the urge to run a finger around his collar. That said, he wasn't going to deny he found the woman attractive. He just didn't need his sister taking that information and running him to the altar before he took another breath. "What is it with newlyweds?"

Ruth blushed. "Fine, fine. I'm just excited. I mean, come on. We lived in D.C. for years and there were only ever dating disasters. Now we're here and I'm married, Mal's engaged, Jonah might as well have a girlfriend, and now you. It's just like everything's falling into place."

"Pretty sure Jonah would disagree with that summary. He says they're just friends. And I've now spoken to Serena twice. I don't think I can even say that much." Micah patted Ruth's hand. She meant well. He'd remind himself of that as often as he needed to. "Please tell me you didn't come over here just because Ursula told you I ate lunch with a woman."

She shrugged. "It's the middle of the afternoon and my only guests checked out this morning. I've got people coming in tomorrow, but for tonight, there's nothing. The rooms are clean, so I figured I might as well head to town and do some errands, one of which was checking up on you."

"And one was the conversation with Ursula about the new features for the B&B website, right? Did she also tell you Jonah is going to do their cake?"

Ruth narrowed her eyes. "I never confirmed it was her. But yes."

Micah chuckled.

"Okay, fine. And yes, but I never doubted Jonah would come around. Still, don't give her a hard time, okay? I had to pry a little. Anyway, I should run." Ruth grinned and turned to leave. She paused by the door and looked back. "Hey, after you talk to Serena about mugs and plates for the bakery, let me know her prices. Having something like that for the B&B would be nicer than the superstore melamine junk Naomi left in the cupboards."

When he talked to her? Micah sighed. He'd said he was thinking about it. He hadn't even mentioned it to Jonah or Mal yet. And they might not want to go that route. Last time they'd talked it over, Jonah was all about making a customized mug with their logo. Malachi had seemed interested in that idea and was supposed to be pricing it out.

Now Micah was going to have to mention this new idea before Ruth said something that got him in trouble. Or...maybe he should check with Serena first and see if it was even something she was interested in. Which wasn't an excuse to get in touch with her. Wasn't it better to have a full picture before bringing the idea to his brothers?

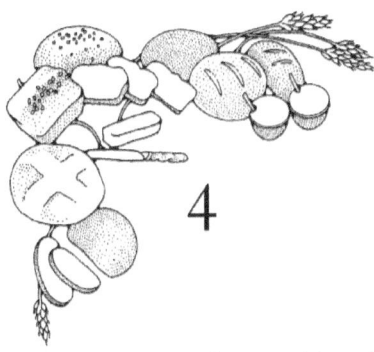

4

The alarm on her phone chimed and Serena turned off her potter's wheel. Thursday mornings could be spent in her studio, but the afternoons were for paperwork. Whether she wanted to get it done or not. The first year she'd been in business, she'd left the paperwork alone until the whim struck. She'd quickly realized that whim was never one she was going to have. Thankfully, her accountant had taken her by the hand and walked her through what needed to be done and when. Now she stuck to that schedule religiously. A small part of her loved seeing the numbers fall into place.

A very small part.

With a sigh, she lifted the pottery bat with her work-in-progress off the wheel and carried it to a table. The slab that attached to her wheel made changing projects so much easier. And it helped with removing pieces when they were ready for glazing, too. She sprayed the pot with water and covered it in plastic. That ought to keep it wet enough that she could continue where she left off later. Maybe tonight. She'd known better than to start something new—usually she stuck to glazing some greenware, coloring clay, or building nerikomi blocks on

Thursday mornings—but today she'd needed the feel of wet clay spinning into a shape that she directed. Hopefully she wouldn't regret it when she got back to the piece.

When her workspace was clean, she grabbed her phone and headed across the gravel driveway to the house, stopping on the deck as Gloria's police cruiser pulled in.

"I brought food." Gloria called as she stepped out of the car and held up a brown paper bag. "I know it's your paperwork afternoon, but I figured you had to eat. Right?"

Serena smiled. "Yeah. Come on in. What'd you bring?"

"Well, since I bailed on you Monday, I figured Jukebox takeout was in order." Gloria climbed the stairs to the deck. "I got you a Reuben."

"Mmm." That ought to hit the spot. Serena pulled open the door and waved her friend in. "Did you know people think I'm dead?"

Gloria crossed the living room to the kitchen island and started unpacking the large brown paper sack of takeout. "Sure. That's an old theory, though. The latest I've seen is alien abduction."

"I'm serious." Serena crossed to the island and perched on a stool.

"So am I. Most of the folks who embrace the alien theory are convinced you're giving acting lessons to a friendly race who want to be sure they can wow us when they finally make widespread contact. Of course they chose you because of your time on *Alien Ninjas.*" Gloria looked at Serena and frowned. "You didn't know?"

Serena shook her head. This is what she got for giving up the gossip circuit when she turned her life over to Jesus. But those blogs and magazines sent her into dangerous waters. It was better—much better—not to have them in her life. "Why do you?"

"Seriously? I'm friends with Serena VanderMay, but I can't tell anyone. So I do the next best thing and read all the conspiracy theories so I can laugh at them from the comfort of my home." Gloria shrugged and popped open the container of French onion soup in front of her. "I'm a little surprised your parents haven't said anything."

"Maybe they have." Serena inhaled the scent of corned beef, sauerkraut, and grilled rye bread. "I don't always listen closely when they start in on their whole 'why don't you come back to Hollywood' spiel."

"So why don't you?" Gloria scooped up a big spoonful of soup. "Not that I want you to go, mind you. But you were poised to transition into bigger films, more grown-up roles, and then *bam* you were gone."

Serena swallowed and ran a finger along the scar on her jaw. "After the accident...it didn't seem likely that I was going to get any of those roles anyway. My scars are too visible. Throw in how hard it is to be a Christian there—particularly on the heels of the life I had been living? No. I'm happier here anyway."

Gloria frowned. "Okay. But for the record, your scars aren't really visible to anyone but you. In fact, I have it on good authority that there's a certain baker in town who happens to think you're hot."

Heat washed over her cheeks. Gloria had to mean Micah. Except wouldn't he have gotten in touch if he was interested? They'd had lunch on Monday. "Yeah? Who's your source? I think they might be mistaken."

"Doubtful. He hasn't called?"

Serena took a bite of her sandwich and shook her head.

"Hmm. Maybe you should stop by. Get a cookie or something." Gloria waggled her eyebrows.

"You're ridiculous. And I've got work here that needs to get done. I'm not disrupting my schedule just because someone may or may not think I'm attractive." Being hot was a far cry from being interesting. Or smart. Or someone he wanted to get to know. All things she'd thought about him the past few days. "How are things with his brother?"

"We're friends, that's all."

"Uh huh. Does he know that?" Serena grinned before taking another bite.

"Of course. He hasn't made any kind of move that would indicate otherwise." Gloria set her spoon down. "I'm not the one who needs more people in her life."

"What is it with everyone? I'm not a hermit. I see people, I get out, but most of all I do my job. I have a busy, active business, in case you hadn't noticed. And pots don't throw themselves."

"Sorry. Your parents on your case again?"

Serena nodded. "Before they left on Saturday, along with the usual suggestion that I should head back to L.A., if only for their Fourth of July party."

"That could be fun."

"No. It really wouldn't." Serena had told Gloria who she was—mostly because her friend had asked straight out—but she didn't know everything. Not even her parents knew the whole story. And it was best if it stayed that way. Going back to L.A. would just reopen all her scars and, well-meaning or not, the questions people asked would undoubtedly reveal entirely too much. "Besides, I'm too busy. I get special orders almost every day now. People seem to like the mixture of techniques I use."

"That's because they're spectacular. The fern-like patterns you get with the coffee thing..."

"Mocha diffusion."

Gloria waved a hand. "Whatever. They're so delicate. People always compliment the mug you made for me. I keep it at the station."

Serena grinned. "I'm glad it's a hit."

The radio on Gloria's shoulder squawked. She bent her head to listen and sighed. "That's my cue. Sorry."

"Don't be. Paperwork calls." Serena stood. "Thanks for lunch."

"You know it. And do me a favor?"

"Sure."

"Swing by Slice of Heaven and say hi to Micah."

She pressed her lips together. "Next time I'm in town."

"Best I'm going to get?"

Serena nodded.

"All right. Later."

Serena stood on the deck and watched Gloria drive off. At least she wasn't running the lights and siren this time, so it must not be too urgent. Her gaze drifted to her studio and her mind filled with the image of the vase she'd started that morning. It wouldn't take that much longer...no. Paperwork had to be done.

Especially if she was seriously thinking about going into town to see a certain handsome baker and ask if he was free for dinner tomorrow night.

Serena pulled the plastic off the vase she'd started that morning and eyed it as she carried it back to her wheel. Paperwork had taken longer than she'd anticipated, and by the time she'd wrapped up, there was no point in trying to catch Micah at the bakery. She could probably call Gloria and get his home address. Or phone number. But it seemed a little over the stalker line to do that. Instead she'd spend some time in the studio, finish her vase, and maybe tomorrow she'd wander into town and see if she couldn't run into Micah.

"Wow."

Serena took her hands off the vase and spun down the potter's wheel before looking up, her heart thundering in her chest. Her gaze landed on Micah and she blinked. Just think of him and he appeared? "Hi."

Micah shifted his weight from one foot to the other. "I knocked, but you were caught up."

She nodded. It happened frequently. Which was why she didn't usually throw pots when she was expecting company. "What brings you up this way?"

"Special delivery." He lifted the small white box he had in his hands and cleared his throat, moving a little closer. "You seemed to enjoy these on Saturday and we had a couple left this evening when we locked up."

"Yeah?" She'd enjoyed all of the bakery treats he'd brought that weekend. What was in the box? Serena wiped her hands on the towel she kept in her lap and stood. "Let's see then."

With a chuckle, Micah handed her the box.

She grinned and flipped open the lid, revealing a small stack of bright pink macarons. "Ooh. These were fantastic. Thanks." Serena studied him for a moment. "Why don't you come inside? I'll make a pot of tea, and we can share."

"I don't want to interrupt more than I already have." Micah gestured to her workspace. "That's...amazing."

Serena turned to look at the wheel. Her latest vase rose nearly three feet from the base to the top, curving into an almost perfect ovoid shape. She'd just finished fluting the lip for a little variety. When it dried, she'd carve shallow rings along the bottom quarter for texture. Overall, she was pleased with it. But amazing seemed a bit too much. "It's coming along. But I'm basically finished. It needs to dry for a few days before I can do more with it. Can you wait a few minutes while I clean up?"

"Sure. Anything I can do to help?"

He was dressed for the bakery in dark jeans and a nice shirt. Nothing formal, but still. "I can't promise you won't get dirty."

He shrugged. "One hundred percent machine washable."

"All right." Serena lifted the bat with her vase attached to it from the wheel. "Can you grab the pan around the wheel and empty it in the sink, then give it a rinse? It pulls apart into two pieces, and I don't think there's enough water in there that it would be a problem."

She slid the vase onto a table and chewed her lower lip. To cover or not, that was the question. With a shrug, she reached for the plastic she'd used earlier that day and made a loose tent. It might take a little longer to get to the leathery stage she needed that way, but the last thing she wanted was for it to crack because it dried unevenly. The shape had turned out better than any of her previous attempts.

"Yuk."

Serena turned, her gaze landing on Micah holding the two halves of the drip pan, the front of his jeans covered in water. She bit back a laugh. "You okay?"

"Oh, yeah. I'm good. I think you might have overestimated my manual dexterity though." Micah shook his head and took the pieces to the sink.

"The latch can be a little tricky. Sorry." Serena took a sponge and wiped up the floor. She crossed to the sink and rinsed it out, ignoring the goose bumps she got standing next to him. After wiping down her wheel and workspace, she carried her sponge and tools back to the sink.

Micah held the clean, dripping halves of the water pan. "Where do I put these?"

Serena nodded to the towel stretched out on the counter. "I keep meaning to buy a drying rack. But the towel works just as well, so..."

"Good enough." He smiled and set the pieces down then stepped out of the way. "Do you ever do custom orders?"

"All the time." She spread her tools out on the towel and turned off the faucet, drying her hands on her jeans. "Need something?"

"Maybe? Have you been into the bakery? I haven't seen you, but I'm not always out front." Micah grabbed the box of cookies off the table.

"Not yet. It was on my list for tomorrow." Serena held open the studio door and waited for Micah to step out. He smelled like a bakery should—that mixture of bread and sugar and coffee—it was better than any cologne she could imagine.

"Was?"

She winced and checked the lock. "I wasn't actually going to visit for the bakery itself. I thought I might stop by and say hi to you."

His eyebrows lifted and one corner of his mouth poked up. "Yeah?"

"Yeah." Serena stepped into the house and gestured toward the sitting area. "Have a seat. I'll put the kettle on."

Micah followed her to the kitchen and leaned against the island. "You can't just leave it there."

"Sure I can." She grinned and held her cobalt blue tea kettle under the tap. He was entirely too much fun to tease. And he could give as well as he took. That was a definite point in his favor. So many guys were willing to flirt and poke fun, but if a girl turned the tables, suddenly they got pouty. Pouting was unattractive on a man. "Tell me about the macarons."

He drummed his fingers on the island while she carried the kettle to the stovetop and turned on the gas. "Okay. First you have to understand there's a difference between a macaron and a macaroon. The second one is basically a sticky ball of coconut. Also, for the record, gross. Now, a macaron, that's a light, meringue-based cookie usually made with ground almonds. In this case, since they're pink, we went with a strawberry jam as the filling. They're one of the few cookies I enjoy playing with, because they have a lot of scope for improvisation."

"You made these?" Hmm. He had said he helped out with the baking when needed. She'd assumed that meant his help was infrequent. "How often do you get in the kitchen?"

"Every morning, for sure. But then I pitch in throughout the day as needed, too. Sometimes we run low on an item or get a special order." He shrugged. "It's just the way it works."

Serena took two mugs down from a cabinet and set them next to the stove. She turned and grabbed the small box she used to hold her tea from the shelf above, flipping it open before she set it next to the mugs. "Do you enjoy it?"

"I do. I like working with my brothers. Most days, at least. And it's nice to know we're brightening some people's lives in the process of making a living." He snagged a tea bag and dropped it into one of the mugs. "These are really nice."

"Thanks. Mugs are always fun. They're easy to throw—relatively—and the surface is easy to play with when it's time to glaze. Something about the cylindrical shape seems to really make the mocha diffusion look like leaves."

"Mocha diffusion?"

When the kettle began to whistle, she flicked off the gas and poured the boiling water over the tea bags. "Sorry. That's a glazing process I frequently use. Basically, you drip an acidic solution onto the slip—that's, effectively, liquid clay that you dip the dried-but-not-fired piece into—and the reaction makes these patterns."

"Interesting." He picked up his tea and turned toward the sitting area.

Serena laughed. "You say that, but your tone implies the exact opposite."

Micah's cheeks reddened. "No. It is interesting. But chemistry was never my thing. So you kind of lost me at 'acidic'."

"Whatever." Serena sat, tucking her legs under her and cradling her mug in her hands. "You bake. That's chemistry."

His eyebrows lifted. "I guess."

"Well, your macarons would suggest you do better than guess." She bit into one of the airy cookies and sighed. They were the perfect blend of crisp and tangy. "What kind of jam did you use?"

"I made it." He shrugged and pulled the teabag from his mug.

Serena pushed a ceramic bowl from the center of the coffee table toward him. "Just drop it in here."

Micah shook his head. "That's too pretty to use for trash. I can just—"

"It's fine. They're all dishwasher safe. I don't bother with things that aren't useful. Usually. I mean, I've made some fancy pieces and decorative ones. But they're not my preference. I like to know things I've made are being enjoyed every day."

"You're sure?" At Serena's nod, Micah dropped the teabag into the bowl. "Anyway, jam's easy. It's basically fruit, sugar, and citrus."

"'Cause it's acidic?"

He chuckled. "Touché."

Serena grinned and nudged the box of cookies toward him. "Aren't you having one?"

"I hadn't planned to. I brought them for you."

"I'm just greedy enough not to push. But I'll leave them on the table in case you change your mind before I eat them all." She eyed him over the top of her mug. "What are we going to do about this?"

"Do?"

He looked genuinely confused. It was adorable. She didn't think she'd misread him though. After all, he was here with cookies for no other discernible reason. "This. You and me?"

Red crawled up his neck to his cheeks and his gaze darted away before slowly returning. "You're very direct."

She shrugged. He wasn't wrong. But she also wasn't going to apologize for something she didn't consider a bad thing. Her entire life had been based on the premise that you went after what you wanted. And you did it with confidence. You didn't survive in Hollywood otherwise. Sure, she wasn't *in* L.A. anymore, but that didn't change the fact that it was a reasonable way to live. "Does that bother you?"

"I'm not sure." He leaned forward and set his scarcely touched tea on the coffee table. "I mostly came by to ask what it would run to have you make maybe twenty mugs, possibly some small plates, too, that we could use at the bakery."

Oh. She took a long drink of tea, willing her stomach to stop twisting. She hadn't misread a cue that badly in a long time. But he didn't need to know that. No one did. Had it been so long since she was attracted to a man that she'd lost her ability to read their interest? "Did you have a design in mind?"

He shook his head. "My brother is tinkering with a logo on a mug—you know the plain white ones with something printed on them you can get everywhere? I wanted something more unique."

"I can't compete with that price."

"Who'd want you to? That's like asking us to sell a loaf of bread for the same buck fifty it costs at the grocery store. Different product, different cost. It's just a matter of knowing what that cost might be."

Serena tapped her finger on the side of her mug before naming a price.

Micah nodded. "That's probably doable. Do you have any sort of advertising cards? Like a postcard or something you'd use at a craft show?"

She snickered before she could stop herself. "I don't do craft shows."

"Okay. I only ask because we figured we could set up a little corner telling about your work over near the mugs. We're doing that for Grant Ward at the Beanery—he's our coffee bean supplier. Anyway, we like to drive business to locals when we can. But it's no biggie." He stood, tucking his hands in his pockets. "I'll get back to you next week. I like the idea, but I have to convince my brothers it's worth the extra expense. How long would it take if we decided to go for it?"

"Just the mugs?"

He nodded.

She could probably throw five mugs a day before making herself crazy and needing to switch to something else. Then they'd need to dry. So she could start glazing the first day's work after she finished the last batch. Then they'd need to be fired. "Maybe two weeks?"

"Nice. Thanks. I'll let you get back to your evening."

"Okay. I'll walk you out."

"You don't have to do that. Just enjoy your cookies." He grinned. "I'll be in touch."

Serena frowned as he pulled the patio door closed behind him. Had she ever been so roundly rejected before in her life? She couldn't drag up any memories of it happening if she had. So. First time for everything?

Or...since they hadn't even known each other a week yet, maybe she'd have to find a way to change his mind.

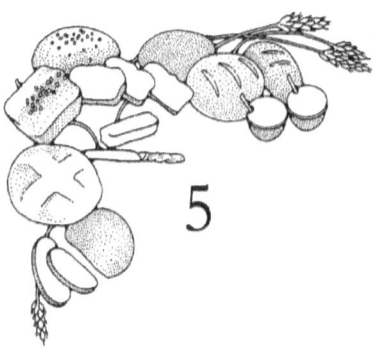

5

"Let me get this straight. You go to her house, bring her cookies, she basically asks you out, and you leave with a quote for mugs." Malachi shook his head. "I'm not sure we're actually related."

"Mal's got a point. Even I wouldn't have managed to screw that up." Jonah tossed a slab of dough onto the counter and began to knead. "But the mugs sound cool. I like the idea of using a local artist."

Malachi frowned. "They're so much more expensive. And they're not really an advertisement for the bakery."

"Yeah, but they're for people to use when they're already *at* the bakery. Why do they need to be an ad?" Micah scooped batter from the giant mixing bowl into muffin tins as he spoke. Everything with Mal ended up being about the bottom line these days. "You're awfully focused on the chance for profit—is there something you're not telling us?"

Malachi shook his head. "No. We're fine. Better than fine, honestly. If that's the route you two want to go, then go for it. Can she do plates, too?"

"I don't see why not, but I didn't specifically ask about those."

"Guess you know your next assignment then." Jonah punched the dough he was working on and dropped it with a plop into a bowl before covering it with a towel and setting it under the counter where it could rise. "And this time, if she asks you out, say yes."

Micah rolled his eyes and continued to scoop the muffin batter into tins. She wasn't going to ask him out—she hadn't really in the first place. And even if she did, was that the kind of woman he wanted to date? He found her attractive. He wouldn't deny it. But he was a reasonably traditional guy. His parents had seen to that, and he didn't have a problem with it. Was it wrong to want to open doors and do the asking when it came to dates? Maybe not modern...but not wrong.

It was probably a moot point. After last night, she was unlikely to want to speak to him again, let alone try and ask him out. Which was too bad. She was the first woman to pique his interest in quite a while.

He carried the muffin tins to the ovens and slid them in before setting the timer. Two more trips got them all loaded. "I'm heading out front to open up. Don't let the muffins burn."

"When have I ever?" Jonah shook his head. "Oh. We're getting rave reviews on the macarons, so think about some variations you can do on them next week. I might like to make them a standard."

A standard? Micah pushed through the door out into the storefront and flipped on the lights. The empty display cases gleamed. They'd be full soon enough. The first batch of bread was nearly ready to come out of the oven, as were the cookies and muffins. Friday was a good day for one-off purchases. They'd get husbands stopping in on their way home from work to grab a loaf of bread for something their wife forgot. Or a box of muffins for a Saturday morning treat. Cookies for an evening get together.

He smiled as he measured fragrant coffee beans into the grinder and punched the button to get it started. Maybe he never imagined living in Idaho, owning a bakery with his brothers, but they were making it work. And it was a pretty good place to be.

There was a tap at the door.

Technically they didn't open for another twenty minutes, but if they had what the customer wanted, a sale was a sale. Micah dusted the coffee grounds off his hands and walked to the front, his steps slowing as he caught sight of her red hair. Serena. She took his breath away. Literally. But looks weren't enough, and he'd remind himself of that as often as he needed to if that's what it took. It sounded like she was a believer though. That was a plus.

With a smile, he flipped the locks on the front door and pushed it open. "Hey. We're not quite set up for the day..."

"I know. Sorry. I wanted to get to you before things got busy." She breezed through the door and slowed, her head swiveling as she took in the space. "This is pretty much what I expected. It even smells like a bakery."

"That's the general idea." He tucked his hands in his pockets to keep from reaching out and touching the one errant curl that flipped in the opposite direction of all the others. "What can I get you?"

"I wouldn't mind some coffee. I had this idea last night after you left and I wanted to show it to you before I spent anymore time playing with it." Serena dug into the enormous bag that was looped over her shoulder and drew out a plastic tub. She pried off the lid and turned the contents out into her hands. "Look."

Micah frowned and studied the block of what he assumed was clay. Centered in the block was a dark brown basket-like shape with golden brown ovals that speared out of it like baguettes frequently did on the top of the display case. But it looked like a solid cube, and he was fairly certain clay didn't actually come with a bakery design in it. "This is cool. How'd you do it?"

"Sometimes I do nerikomi—it's a Japanese technique where you build blocks of clay, different colors and shapes, to make designs. This was more complex than I've tried before. Usually I stick with curlicues, sunbursts, checkerboards, that sort of thing. But I got the picture in my head and couldn't sleep until I at least tried. You like it?"

"It's amazing. How would you make it into mugs?"

Serena blew out a breath. "I'm not sure if I can. I'd typically use it for something flat like plates or a platter, maybe a decorative wall piece. I've seen people use it for hollow items before though, so I know it can be done. It just might take me a bit longer."

"Plates? Like little ones for a cookie?" Micah held his hands in the shape of a dessert plate.

She nodded.

"We'd like some of those, too."

"Okay. Those I can for sure do with this pattern. Do you want me to try the mugs?"

Micah studied her face. Her cheeks were flushed and her eyes sparkled. Three puckered pinkish-red scars stood out in direct contrast to her otherwise flawless skin. How had he never noticed them before? "Do you want to?"

"I really do. I just—it's going to change the time estimate. I might not be able to get them done in two weeks."

"That's okay. For this? Totally worth the wait. What happened to your face?"

Serena flinched as if she'd been struck.

"Sorry. I—it's just..." He clamped his mouth shut. One of these days he really was going to master the idea of thinking before speaking.

"No. It's fine. I forgot I didn't put on makeup. I was too excited to show you this. I was in a bad accident several years ago. I don't really talk about it." Serena cleared her throat. "So. I'll do the plates for sure and see if I can make mugs work. If I can't, do you just want to cancel that portion of the order?"

Micah shook his head. "No. We still want your mugs. Just make something that goes along with the plates. I'm really sorry. My tongue gets ahead of my brain."

"Don't mention it. Seriously." Her smile was tight as she turned to go.

He couldn't let her leave mad—or upset—whatever she was. "Can I get you a muffin or something? They should be coming out of the oven in just a minute. Or that coffee you wanted?"

"I'm not sure that's a good idea. I have work I should be getting back to." She held up the block of clay before lowering it carefully back into the container and affixing the lid. "Besides, you're not open yet, right?"

"Door's unlocked. Coffee's almost ready. Baking is nearly done." Micah shrugged and struggled to keep his voice casual. "That's basically open. We have carrot cake cookies today."

She wrinkled her nose. "I can't even imagine how that would be good."

He laughed and held up a finger. "Wait right there. Okay? Please?"

Micah dashed into the kitchen. The baskets and trays for the display cases were filled and lined up on the counter nearest the door.

"About time. You get lost on the way to the coffee pot?" Jonah brought another load of bread over and set it down.

"Serena's here. She had this cool idea for the mugs that she wanted to show me. Where are the cookies?"

Jonah's eyebrows lifted as he pointed to the tray practically in front of Micah. "Don't forget to get the rest of the case set up."

Waving his brother off, Micah picked up the cookies for the display and pushed through the door. He let out his breath. She was still here. "Prepare to be amazed."

"That's setting the bar kind of high, isn't it? Let's go for not revolted."

"Oh ye of little faith." Micah grinned and slid the tray into its spot in the display case before pulling a sheet of tissue paper from a box and using it to grab a cookie. "That's cream cheese icing sandwiched between them."

"Of course it is." Serena eyed the treat before accepting it. "People like these?"

This was only the second time they'd featured this particular cookie. It wasn't a runaway best seller or anything, but it did okay. "They do. Want some coffee?"

"Might as well." Serena pulled out a chair and sat. She placed the cookie in front of her and poked the top. "Cream and sugar if you have it."

"Real sugar? Agave? Honey? Fake sugar?" Micah held an insulated disposable cup under the dispenser and breathed in the rich aroma of the dark liquid.

"That's an awful lot of options for a place where coffee is just a sideline. I'll live on the edge and use the real stuff." She broke off a tiny piece of cookie and sniffed it before popping it into her mouth. Her lips curved up.

"See? Good, right?" Micah set the coffee in front of her and dropped down across from her at the small table. *Don't focus on the scars.* He dropped his gaze to her lips. They were full and pink. Imminently kissable. Maybe being accused of staring at the scars was a better idea after all.

Serena broke off a larger piece and popped it in her mouth. "I have to give you this one. It's not quite what I expected. That's a good thing."

"I'm glad." His throat was suddenly dry. "Do you—"

"Are you ever going to load the cases?" Jonah poked his head through the swinging door and winced. "Sorry."

"It's okay. Serena, this is my brother, Jonah. He's the primary baker here at A Slice of Heaven."

"Hi. Nice to meet you. I'm sorry for keeping your brother away from his work. If you have a lid, I can take this to go." Serena pushed her chair back and stood.

"You don't have to. Just sit." Micah stood and glared over his shoulder at Jonah. "I can load the cases while you enjoy. There's no hurry."

"If you're sure."

Micah nodded.

"Okay." Serena sat and took a long drink of coffee. "This is good, too."

Jonah laughed. "You sound surprised."

"In my experience, bakery coffee isn't always the best."

Jonah moved out of the way so Micah could get past him and to the kitchen where he could grab the first load of bread for the cases. Serena was laughing when he returned to the front of the shop. Was his brother not going to help?

Micah set the basket of bread on top of the case and went back for more. Jonah was doing his charming thing again and flirting. He was shameless.

"All the bread has been moved off your counter, oh mighty one." Micah fought the urge to stick his tongue out at his brother. If Serena wasn't still at the table, he totally would have.

Jonah cocked his head to the side. "You haven't had any coffee yet, obviously."

Whatever. Micah started arranging the shelves in the display case with today's offerings.

Serena stood. "Thanks for the cookie. And the coffee. What do I owe you?"

"It's on me." Micah's smile was weak. They'd been having a good time. It wasn't like there was a line down the block waiting to get in as soon as they opened. Now she was leaving and he hadn't worked out whether or not he was going to ask her out. If she'd even accept at this point.

"Well. Thanks." Serena moistened her lips and studied Micah for two long heartbeats. She took one of their business cards from beside the cash register and a pen from the cup and scribbled on the back before offering it to Micah. "If you need to ask me anything, here's my cell. Otherwise, the plates will be about two weeks. The mugs...I'll have to let you know."

She was out the door before a coherent thought formed in his brain. Micah looked down at the seven digits on the card. She had good handwriting.

"Nice." Jonah nudged Micah in the ribs. "You have to call and ask her out. She came into town just to see you."

"How do you get that? She wanted to show me the nakamushi—or whatever the technique is called—clay."

Jonah shook his head. "It's really sad that my brothers are both idiots where women are concerned. If that was the only thing she wanted to do, she would have emailed you a picture like she does with other clients."

"How do you know?" There was no way that was true.

"Because I casually asked about her designs and she was more than happy to show me the photos on her phone and explain how she does exactly that with most of her custom-order clients." Jonah grinned. "In fact, she had a picture of the bread basket in there. She had to do a little tap dancing to explain why she hadn't sent it."

"I—"

"Need to think about it. I know." Jonah punched Micah's shoulder. "Don't take too long. I like her. She looks a lot like that actress you used to moon over, but she's also fun to talk to and still alive, which is a bonus."

"I don't buy those rumors." Micah closed his eyes. That was a testament to how off his game he was if that slipped out.

"Ah-ha! You still have a crush on her. That's hilarious and yet kind of pathetic at the same time." Jonah shook his head. "Do yourself a favor. Take a step toward a normal life instead of one steeped in unrealistic fantasy, and ask Serena out."

"I'll think about it." As the door chimed and the first morning pickup bustled in, Micah snapped his mouth closed on further comment. Which just as well. Taking orders and making change were things he understood. Women...were usually safer when left completely in the imagination.

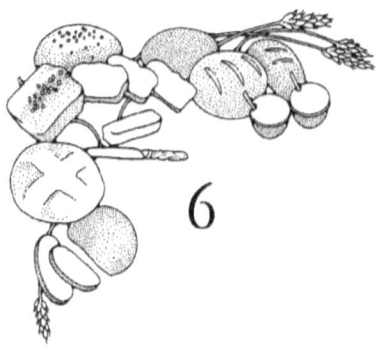

6

Serena set the block of clay containing her bakery design on one of her work tables and used fishing line and thin strips of wood to slice off pieces. She tucked each slice under a wet cloth before returning to the block. It wouldn't do for them to dry out while she got all the cutting done. When she had twenty of them, she spritzed what remained of the block with water and tucked it back into the plastic tub and turned to rolling out the first plate.

Was he ever going to call?

She blew the hair out of her eyes. It didn't matter. *Wouldn't* matter. She'd given him two chances. He was either interested or he wasn't. It certainly seemed like the latter, which was too bad. Micah was fun to talk to. His brother, Jonah, wasn't bad either. But she hadn't felt that same pull she did with Micah. He was interesting and challenging—it'd been a while since a man didn't immediately return the interest she showed—at the same time. It didn't hurt that he was good looking, either. She hadn't been drawn to a man like that since Derrick.

Serena closed her eyes and drew in a deep breath as her chest tightened. Was it ever going to get easier?

The books said it would. So did her counselor. She was still waiting for it to be true. Better, at least for now, to close off those memories and focus on what she did have. She had her studio, clients who came back and commissioned new pieces, and a handful of friends here in Arcadia Valley. If Micah Baxter didn't want to be part of that, well, that was his problem.

Her gaze flitted to her cell phone. It sat on the table, its blank screen mocking her. She should have turned on music like she usually did. But she hadn't wanted to miss any calls. She groaned and forced herself to look down at the rolled-out clay. She'd focus on the plates and leave the rest to God.

Snagging one of the square slices of the nerikomi block from under the wet cloth, Serena smoothed it onto the clay that would form the platter's base and covered the whole thing with cloth. She'd roll them until they were one cohesive unit, cut the final shape, form the edges of the plate, and then set it aside to dry. Then she'd repeat the process, and maybe, if she was lucky, it would keep her mind off Micah and whether or not he was as interested in her as she was in him.

The crick in her back told her it was time for a break. Serena stretched and strode to the sink to wash her hands. She had half of the plates made. That was something. Maybe after lunch she'd finish the batch and get them drying. With all the blended clays, they'd need to dry covered. It took longer, but it helped keep them from cracking when she fired them.

She tapped her phone to check the time and winced. Nearly two. That's what happened when she got absorbed in a project. And her thoughts. Maybe she'd spend a few minutes catching up on email while she ate. She tucked her phone in her pocket and left the studio.

Summer heat assaulted her as she crossed the driveway to her house. It wasn't overwhelming today at least. She'd slap a sandwich together and sit on the deck. Most of her email could be handled on her phone anyway, and the sunlight would do her good. That was probably the only thing she missed about California. The beach. Sunshine nearly every day. Driving her convertible on the Pacific Coast Highway with the wind in her hair and the smell of the surf surrounding her.

The phone's buzzing jolted her out of her memories. "Hello?"

"Serena, dear, it's Mom."

She winced. That's what she got for not checking the display before answering. She still would've picked up, but preparation was always better when it came to her mother. "Hi. What's up?"

"We're taking an early lunch and I thought I'd check in. Your father and I had a lovely time this past weekend. It was so nice to see you. Are you *sure* you can't make it out for the Fourth?"

"I enjoyed seeing you, too. I appreciate you making the trip." Using her shoulder to hold her phone to her ear, Serena pulled two slices of bread out and frowned into the refrigerator. Looked like it was cheese and tomato. Again. She really needed to up her sandwich game.

"And the party?"

"Mom...I just can't. I'm sorry. I know it disappoints you." She fended off the stab of guilt that came with the words. She didn't mean to let her parents down, but that wasn't her life now. Serena grabbed the small jar of mayonnaise and moved to the island to assemble her lunch.

Her mother sighed. "Jerry has a script he wants you to read. I was hoping you could talk to him about it then. I'll just give him your email."

"No." Her heart pounded. A script from Jerry was tempting—very tempting—but she was done with that life. Wasn't she? "Have him send it through Zennia."

"I thought you fired her. You still keep her on as your agent?"

Serena spread mayo on the bread before layering slices of tomato followed by cheese. Technically her mother was right. She wasn't actively represented by anyone anymore. "We're friends. She'll still pass things on. I'll let her know it's coming."

"Fantastic. It'll be so good to have you back in town doing what you were born to do."

"Mom. Looking at a script is a far cry from auditioning and landing the part." She closed her eyes. Maybe she should tell Zennia to wait two days and then just tell Jerry she wasn't interested.

"Please. Jerry says the part's custom-made for you. If you want it, it's yours. And it would open the door to so many new opportunities. Isn't it time to let people know, once and for all, that you're not dead?"

Serena's stomach sank. "You knew about that?"

"Of course, didn't you? There are so many ridiculous theories out there, but that's the one that gets the most attention. Your father and I fought it at first, but it only seemed to make it worse, so now we just stay out of it. You did such a good job disappearing after you got out of the hospital, I guess we figured it's what you wanted."

"Thanks. And no, I only heard that one this week."

"Darling, you need to stay current if you're coming back. I'll get your subscriptions to the industry magazines updated. You should let the guild know your new address, too. Or I'll do it—I'll be seeing—"

Serena's chest constricted, making it hard to breathe. "Stop. You know what? This is a bad idea. Just tell Jerry I'm flattered, but I'm happy here. I don't need a comeback role when I have no interest in making a comeback."

"But—"

"No. Mom. Just...no. I'm sorry. I know it's disappointing and that you don't understand. But can you please trust me?" She rubbed her chest, just over her heart.

"I don't understand you, Serena. You could have everything back. It'd be like you never left."

Serena mumbled something and ended the call. Maybe she could get her career back—and even that was an iffy proposition—but it would never be like it was before. Before, there'd been Derrick. Now he was dead.

Serena looked up from her work table and frowned.

"Hi. Am I interrupting?"

She fought to keep the frown from turning into a scowl. "Not really. Come on in."

Micah crossed the studio, hands tucked loosely in his pockets. "I tried to call, but you didn't answer. So I thought I'd swing by and see if you wanted to grab a bite."

After her mother's call, she'd turned the phone off. Usually that was a hint that someone wasn't in the mood to talk. Not even to handsome, interesting men. Apparently Micah hadn't gotten the memo. "What time is it?"

"Almost six thirty. We close the bakery at five thirty and there's clean up and stuff to do, so..." He shrugged. "Is it too late?"

Serena stared down at the block of clay she was building as an experiment for the bakery's mugs and fought to get her attitude under control. She'd been upset that he hadn't called, and now, here he was. This was a good thing. "No, it's fine. I need to finish this and get it started drying first though. Then clean up. I'll probably be close to an hour?"

"That's fine." He wandered over to one of the shelves that held pottery in the process of drying before being glazed and fired. "Mind if I hang? Or I can come back."

She rolled the lighter brown clay that represented the baguettes into a tube and fitted it against the block, pressing and pinching until it was the right shape and joined to the clay around it. Did she mind? She didn't usually let people watch her work. Unlike acting, making pottery was trickier when people were around. But he was here. If she said he had to go, he'd barely have time to do anything when he got back to town before he had to turn around. Or she could offer to just meet him somewhere. But... "Sure. You can go in the house, if you want. It's more comfortable. The TV remote's on the coffee table, but I only have streaming. Still, there's probably something on."

"Would you prefer that?" He ambled closer to her work space and peered down at the clay before holding her gaze.

Her breath caught in her lungs. The man was potent. She hadn't been wrong about their chemistry. Serena managed a nod. "Do you mind?"

Micah grinned. "Nope. But I might just sit out on your deck. It's a nice June evening and I have a book with me in the car. Take your time."

She watched him leave before returning to her project. He had a book in the car. Who did that? It was smart. She always intended to pack something for unexpected delays, although it was unlikely to be a book—but a magazine would count, right? He'd probably been in some kind of wilderness club as a kid—didn't they have a saying about always being prepared?

Her gaze darted up. She could just see him on the deck, his feet up on the rail, a book in his lap, perfectly at home. Serena blew out a breath. Just because he'd said to take her time didn't mean she should dawdle. She arranged the next segment of clay and banged the block on the table to meld them. When she was satisfied with the design, she added solid colors of clay to each side and repeated the process of whacking the block on the table to bind the materials together. This one had more of the solid color on top and bottom than the example she'd taken to the bakery that morning. If all went well, after it had time to dry, she could carve it into a mug on the wheel. She'd do one as an experiment before committing to the rest of the order.

Serena set the clay to dry and tidied her workspace before stepping out of the studio and locking the door. Micah appeared engrossed in his book. The sunlight filtered through the trees and brought out the different shades of brown in his hair. She climbed the steps of the deck. "I'll just be another few minutes."

He looked up and smiled. "Okay."

Shaking her head, Serena stepped into the house and hurried back to her bedroom. Glancing in the mirror over the sink she stopped, eyes wide. Her hair was stuck to her head on one side where she'd clearly run her hand through it. Clay was an amazing glue. Especially for hair. She'd never bothered with makeup, and her scars...one made a glaring red line from her ear, along her jaw, then up to the corner of her mouth. Another wiggled from her hairline to her right eye, by the bridge of her nose.

He'd seen her like this and still asked her out?

She was a long way from Hollywood.

Serena stepped under the spray of her shower and tried to imagine what her parents would have to say about her appearance. The words escaped her. Then again, maybe they wouldn't say anything. They'd be too appalled to speak. The first memory she had in the hospital after the accident was her mother trying to apply foundation around her bandages, as if that was somehow going to fix everything. It had been a relief to everyone when Serena had insisted she was fine and had sent them back to work.

Clean and dressed in jeans and a casual T-shirt, Serena gathered her hair into a ponytail and quickly fixed her face. She couldn't make the lines disappear completely, but she could mask them well enough that the casual observer didn't notice. Or if they noticed, they weren't obvious enough to need to be remarked upon. She checked the time on her phone and slid her feet into low-heeled sandals. Just over an hour. Well, she'd warned him.

He didn't look as if he'd moved an inch. "Ready?"

Micah tucked a bookmark between the pages and stood, a smile spreading over his face. "Yeah. You look nice."

"I clean up pretty well."

He chuckled. "Any preferences for dinner? I'd been thinking of L'Aubergine. I haven't made time to try it yet—didn't seem like the kind of place you go alone from what Mal and Ruth have said—but we might not be dressed for it."

"Probably not." She could change easily enough. But would he want to go back to his place and extend their meal even more? "Casual is fine. I've eaten at every place in town and like them. So really, whatever is fine."

"Hmm. I could go for a Reuben, then. Jukebox okay?"

She grinned. "Always. Their fries...I can't get enough of them."

"You should try the onion rings sometime." Micah pulled open the passenger door to his car and held it for her.

Serena gave him a long look before she sat. Who held doors open anymore? She reached for the handle as he pushed the door shut. Huh. She watched him circle around to the driver's side and fastened her seatbelt. "I have used doors before."

"Okay. If that's going to bother you, maybe we should just call it a day. My mother ingrained into all of us that courtesy—which includes doing things like opening and holding doors—isn't optional. It's also not an indication that I think you're incapable. Why do people jump to that conclusion? It was like that a lot in D.C., too." Micah buckled his seatbelt but made no move to start the car. "Why isn't the immediate response along the lines of 'Thank you. That was kind.'?"

Heat seared her cheeks. It was a valid question. *Was* there a reason her reaction was always negative? "Sorry."

"It's okay. I'd really like to know, though."

"I'll have to think about it. In the meantime, I'll work on not letting it bother me if you won't be offended if I open a door when I get to it first."

Micah chuckled and started the car. "Deal. So. Onion rings?"

"Only if you're having some." Onions didn't seem like the thing to eat on a date. And this was definitely a date. She could make a case either way for the pizza lunch having been a date—maybe he was just been being kind when he paid for hers—but this had all the date indicators.

"Oh, yeah. I never skip the rings at the Jukebox. Reuben and rings. It's my go-to meal there."

She laughed. "I wouldn't have thought you'd go for a sandwich. You're surrounded by bread all day."

"True. But this is bread I didn't make. Although, they've talked to us a couple of times about collaboration. We're not sure how to manage the production and keep the quality where we want it. Jonah's thinking things through. If anyone can find a way, it'll be him."

What would it be like to have siblings? "There are four of you, right? You like it?"

"Yeah. It has its moments, of course. Sometimes the three of them get an idea and gang up on you until you cave and drive somewhere to ask a woman to dinner, for example."

Was he joking? He had to be, right? "Hypothetically speaking, I'm sure."

He shook his head and turned into the Jukebox parking lot. It was busy—not crazily—but they certainly wouldn't have the place to themselves. He cast a side-eye glance in her direction. "I was going to get around to it."

"I'll have to send them a thank you note." After he parked, she pushed open her door before he had a chance to ask her to wait while he came to get it. There were limits. There had to be. "For what it's worth, I'm glad you did."

Micah smiled. "So am I."

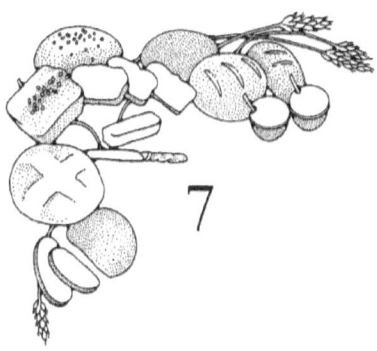

7

Micah held the door for Serena. She was clearly fighting to keep from rolling her eyes, but he couldn't help it. "I know, I know, you're perfectly capable."

"Two, please." Serena glanced over her shoulder. "Or was I supposed to let you say that, too?"

He sighed. "Nope. You're good."

On the one hand, she had a smart mouth and wasn't afraid to use it. It was a nice change from the quiet girls who were too worried about what he'd think to say how they really felt about something until they'd been together for several weeks—and then only after he'd done something wrong without knowing it. On the other hand, was he ever going to stop making missteps? He was doing the best he could.

"Right this way." The hostess made a mark on the podium seating chart, collected two plastic-coated menus, and started off toward the far side of the restaurant.

Micah followed behind Serena. Maybe he should've elbowed her aside and gone first just to prove he didn't think she was incapable of bringing up the rear, but it seemed rude.

When they were seated in a booth, Serena flipped her menu open on the table top. "It's busier than I thought it'd be."

"What's better than a milkshake on Friday night?" Micah shrugged. He probably spent too many Friday nights at the Jukebox. But it was good to get out of the house and Ruth and Corban's ham-handed attempts to set him up with random women from church. Jonah solved the problem by disappearing into his room, but Micah couldn't bring himself to be that way. So he'd sat through quite a few awkward "game nights" that "just happened to pop up."

"You have a point. Hmm. Does a milkshake go with onion rings?"

"Absolutely."

"Micah?" Pamela Hadley and her husband, friends of Corban and Ruth, paused at their table. "We haven't seen you in a while. Ruth says you've been keeping to yourself."

He cleared his throat. "Just trying to stay under the radar. Where are the boys?"

"My parents are babysitting." Emerson reached out and shook Micah's hand. "Date night is easy when you've got family in town."

"Nice. Tell the boys I said hi and that I'm going to crush them the next time they're over. I've been practicing my video game driving skills and don't fall off the track nearly as often anymore." Micah caught Pamela's pointed look at Serena and fought a sigh. "This is Serena Johnson. Serena, this is Pamela and Emerson

Hadley. They're friends of Corban who went ahead and adopted the rest of us when he and my sister got married."

Pamela laughed. "Like that was a hardship. It's so nice to meet you. I hope it's not weird when I say I've been a big fan for forever. Emerson can tell you all about how I've been scheming to meet you in person."

"It's true." Emerson grinned. "You have no idea how many close calls you've had."

"That's never weird and always a pleasure. I wish you hadn't felt like you shouldn't come and introduce yourself though." Serena scooted over, making room in the booth. "Why don't you join us?"

Micah looked between the two women. What was going on? He turned to Emerson. "She's a big pottery fan?"

Emerson shook his head. "You're sure you don't mind?"

Micah minded. A lot. He opened his mouth to object.

"Of course not." Serena patted the seat.

Heart sinking, Micah made room for Emerson on the booth. "Can someone help me out? I'm a little lost."

"Seriously?" Pamela laughed.

Micah shrugged.

"Maybe you know the name Serena VanderMay better?" Serena straightened the wrapped silverware in front of her before meeting his gaze.

It was a jolt. He'd seen the resemblance and dismissed it as a coincidence. There were a lot of pretty redheads in the world. But...no way. "You're her? Johnson is...?"

"My real last name. It's not a secret. Pretty sure my Wikipedia page even has a link to my pottery website." Serena shrugged. "I just don't call attention to it if I can avoid it."

"Oh. Sorry." Pamela winced. "I never even thought—"

"Don't be silly. I don't mind." Serena's gaze locked with Micah's. "Close your mouth."

Micah snapped his teeth together. He was on a date with Serena VanderMay? There was absolutely no way to process that right now. He pushed the knowledge deep into his mind and wiped his palms on his jeans. "Okay. So. Should we order?"

"How was the date?" Jonah slipped a scrap of paper between the pages of his book and set it aside as Micah kicked the door of the farmhouse closed and toed off his shoes.

Micah crossed to the living room and dropped onto the couch. "Did you know?"

"Know what?"

He studied his brother's face. Jonah had tells when he was hiding something. None of them were evident. That helped a little. Very little. Did Malachi and Ruth know? Both of them had mentioned his crush. Could it possibly be coincidence? "It's her."

"Serena is her...? I'm so lost." Jonah leaned forward. "Let's start over. How was your date?"

Micah groaned. "Good. I guess. Pam and Emerson were at the Jukebox, too. They ended up sitting with us."

"Hmm. Sometimes having other people around keeps the conversation flowing. Still, it was a little strange for them to horn in on your date."

"Serena invited them to join us after Pam started gushing about how she was a huge fan." Micah watched Jonah closely. If his brother knew, he was doing a great job hiding it.

"She's a pottery fan? That's...weird. I mean, Serena's talented, but a fan?"

"Exactly. I said something along those lines and Serena's all 'Maybe you'd know me better as Serena VanderMay.'"

"No way."

Micah smiled. His brother looked about like he probably had at the restaurant. "Pretty much. And close your mouth."

"You went on a date with Serena VanderMay. *The* Serena VanderMay? Dude." Jonah shook his head. "How'd we miss that?"

"I did point out the resemblance. But why would she be *here*?" Arcadia Valley wasn't exactly the scene anyone would associate with the media-loving, no-holds-barred, just on the edge of bad girl Serena VanderMay. Micah sighed. How was he supposed to reconcile the Serena he'd been getting to know with the girl who'd lived her life on the front page of every skeezy tabloid? "And maybe that's the point."

"New place, new life?" Jonah grinned. "Sounds like the four of us. Did you ask her?"

"No. It didn't seem like the time and place. Especially not with Pam and Emerson sitting there. I don't know."

Jonah frowned. "What?"

"You know the major thing I had for her as a teenager. But you're not supposed to have the chance to get to know a celebrity crush. They're fantasies for a reason." Micah shook his head. Who actually got the chance to date the famous person they imagined themselves in love with? Other famous people, that's who. Not some random guy who quit working with kids to help his brothers open a community-supported bakery.

The front door opened and Malachi kicked off his shoes before closing it behind him. He looked up and his grin turned into a frown. "Why are you home already, Micah?"

"Good to see you, too, bro."

Jonah laughed. "We could ask you the same thing. You were on a date with your fiancée, I'm pretty sure those are supposed to last longer than first dates."

Malachi's cheeks turned a bright shade of red. "I...needed to come home."

"Are you sick?" Micah stood. "Sit down. I'll go make some tea. Or do you need soup?"

"I'm not sick." Malachi crossed the room and plopped into a chair. "But your concern is touching, even if I'm pretty sure it's just a diversionary tactic."

His brother didn't look sick. Micah frowned. "Did you make Ursula mad?"

Malachi made a strangled sound. "No. She's fine. We're fine. We're just...ready to be married. And until we are, we agreed that our dates needed to be in public places or with friends. Or maybe both. Since neither of those were the case tonight, I needed to come home."

"Oh." Micah grinned, even as a little pang of something—couldn't be jealousy, could it?—hit him mid-chest. "Got it."

"And so we return to my previous question: why are *you* home so early?" Malachi wriggled to get more comfortable before propping his feet on the coffee table and pinning Micah with his gaze.

Micah shrugged and related the date, this time with Jonah interspersing pithy comments throughout.

"Huh."

"That's it? That's all you've got to say?" Micah shook his head. "Thanks. That's very helpful."

"I try." Malachi smiled and held up his hand before Micah could say anything. "If we take the whole celebrity crush out of it, I guess I'm still confused. You like her. You have interesting conversations. You find her attractive. So what's the problem?"

Where did he even start? She was from a completely different world. She'd been hooked up with Derrick King before he died, and that didn't take into account all the other names—big names—she'd dated less seriously. Serena had spent her childhood in front of the camera, whether she was working or on her own time, and from what he'd read, she always acted like she enjoyed it. Craved it, even. Micah, on the other hand, had always wanted the simple, straightforward life his parents had. A steady, solid marriage and family where love just simply was, without question. How did two people from such vastly different upbringings find common ground?

"We're from two different worlds."

Malachi nodded. "Maybe so. But she's here, now, isn't she?"

She was. But how long could someplace like Arcadia Valley hope to hold her?

Malachi's elbow dug into Micah's ribs. Micah turned and hissed at his brother. "Ow. How old are you?"

Malachi jerked his head toward the back of the sanctuary.

Micah looked, freezing when his gaze landed on Serena hesitating in the doorway, her eyes scanning the crowd.

"Go." Mal's elbow struck again. "You know she's here for you."

"I don't know that at all."

Ursula leaned around Malachi and frowned. "Are you really that big of an idiot? Go."

Hunching his shoulders, Micah stood and slid out of the row. He tucked his hands in his pockets as he strode down the aisle toward Serena. What if he was right and she wasn't looking for him? He was going to look like an fool. He cleared his throat. "Hey."

Serena grinned. "Hi. I was hoping I'd see you. It's more crowded than I imagined."

"We're a good-sized church, even if we only have one service." Why was he defensive? He'd had the same thought the first couple of times he'd come with his sister. But still.

"I wasn't trying to be disparaging." Serena sighed. "Maybe this was a bad idea."

Micah took a deep breath and shook his head. "Why don't you tell me what the idea was, and I'll let you know."

A smile played at the corners of her lips. "I realized I hadn't apologized for asking your friends to join us on Friday, and I wanted to do that. I also thought maybe I could make it up to you with lunch after church?"

He nodded slowly, though it rubbed him the wrong way for her to ask him out. Serena was clearly a woman who said what she thought and asked for what she wanted. And wasn't that better than playing games and expecting him to figure it out? "Definitely not a bad idea."

She grinned, her breath coming out in a light whoosh. "Excellent."

"Let's get a seat—they should be starting any minute." Micah glanced toward where his family was sitting. Did he want to subject her to that? Of course, if he didn't, he'd never hear the end of it. "My family's all up front...I'm fine either way, but I know they'd like it if you'd join us."

"Sure. Lead the way." Serena grabbed his hand with a smile.

His fingers reflexively tightened around hers. There was something there. Was it worth pursuing? He reached the row where his family sat as the music started. He'd have to pray about it—a lot.

The service was good. At least what parts of it he could concentrate on. Serena's presence was a like a beacon, drawing and holding his attention regardless of his attempts to pay attention to the sermon. He'd forced himself to take notes during the message. Though he usually preferred to sit and absorb, his mind wouldn't focus without the pen in his hand. At least this way he could read them over at home and try to get more— something?—out of it.

As they stood for the benediction, Serena's hand once again found his. He smiled and wove his fingers through hers.

"Hi Serena, it's good to see you again." Jonah waved from where he sat at the far end of the row.

Serena lifted a hand. "Hi."

Micah cleared his throat. "You haven't met my brother Malachi yet, I don't think. And his fiancée,

Ursula. And my sister, Ruth, and her husband, Corban, are around here somewhere. Or they were."

"Ruth got a text halfway through the sermon. I'm guessing it's something at the B&B." Jonah scooted closer. "They snuck out. You going to join us for lunch, Serena?"

"Oh. Um." Serena turned to meet Micah's gaze.

Micah shook his head. "I think we're going to head out on our own. I'll catch you guys back at home."

"Nice to meet you." Serena lifted a hand before turning and edging out into the aisle, her hand reaching again for Micah's.

He wouldn't have pegged her for the touchy-feely type. Was she nervous? Insecure? Whatever it was, he wasn't going to complain. He could easily get used to the contact. "Did you have a place in mind? A lot of folks from church end up at the Sunrise Café, so..."

"I make a mean omelet. If you're interested?"

His eyebrows lifted. That would definitely keep them from being interrupted again. Was it too secluded? Did she have more than breakfast in mind? No. Everything pointed to her having turned her life around. "Sure. That sounds good. I'll meet you at your place?"

"That works. See you in a few." She squeezed his hand before heading off toward her car.

Micah frowned. He'd planned to at least walk her over.

"She's pretty." Ursula smiled. "She doesn't usually go here, does she? That hair is hard to miss."

Micah shook his head. "She goes to Arcadia Valley Community."

"So she came today to find you?" Malachi waggled his eyebrows. "Maybe your date Friday wasn't as terrible as you thought."

"Apparently not. Anyway. She's making me lunch."

"Yeah?" Malachi chuckled. "That's one way to keep you to herself."

Or for things to get very awkward very fast. Only time would tell. "I should get going. I don't want her to think I'm standing her up. If you check in on Ruth, would you text me and let me know she's okay? It's not like her to leave church."

Ursula chuckled. "The two of you are a pair. We're on our way over to the B&B right now. We figure if everything's okay, we can probably squeeze a meal out of Ruth. And if not, we're there to help. But we'll let you know. Enjoy your lunch."

Micah headed out into the parking lot, offering a few waves to people he knew as he passed. Lunch with Serena. At her house. She was interested in him, that much was obvious, and despite some misgivings, he wanted to see where—if anywhere—it could go. Was it possible to have a regular relationship with someone like her?

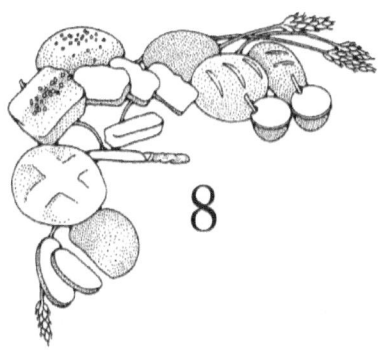

8

Serena pressed a hand to her stomach. She hadn't cooked for a man since Derrick. She squeezed her eyes shut. It was time—past time—to move on. Five years was plenty. Derrick would've been the first to say so. She slipped the chain holding the locket she'd had made from their wedding rings out from under her blouse and rubbed it. Moving on didn't mean forgetting.

She opened the fridge and got out the produce she'd picked up at the farmers market the day before. Micah should be here any minute—he'd probably been stopped by people he knew as he was leaving. Should she have offered to drive him? Then she would have had to bring him back to the church to get his car—or he to get hers, if he'd driven—and that simply hadn't made sense. Whatever. It didn't matter now.

She glanced up at the knock on the glass door and beckoned Micah in. "Anything you don't like in your omelet?"

Micah tucked his hands in his pockets and sauntered to the kitchen island. He tapped the bell pepper. "Not a huge fan, but a little's okay."

"Got it. Want to help chop?"

He shrugged. "Sure. Since I already know my way around your kitchen."

Serena laughed. "Do I need to apologize? Kiln openings make me crazy. Throw in my parents coming, and I was a mess."

"It's all good." Micah scrubbed his hands at the sink. "Where's your towel?"

"Here." She flipped the kitchen towel off her shoulder and handed it to him. "Grab a knife. Any vegetable preference?"

"I'll do the mushrooms. Did you clean them yet?"

Serena handed him the package. "Not yet."

Micah took them to the sink and wet the corner of the towel. He started wiping the mushrooms, setting the cleaned ones in a pile on the counter. "How'd you like Grace?"

"It was good. I can see why you go there." She wasn't ready to leave Arcadia Valley Community, but if Micah needed her to down the road...what was she thinking? It was a long jump from lunch together—a second date, third maybe if you counted pizza—to the kind of future that put them at church together every week. Waking up together. "I was married to Derrick King."

Micah dropped the mushroom he was holding and turned. "What?"

She squeezed her eyes shut. One of these days she needed to learn to think before she spoke. "Derrick and I were married. No one knew. We hadn't figured out when—or how—we were going to announce it. Four months. We eloped four months before the accident. I thought you deserved to know."

"Okay." He looked back at the mushrooms. "Diced or sliced."

Diced or sliced? That was it? No questions. Okay. "Um. Diced, I guess."

Micah slid a cutting board from behind her knife block and began to dice the mushrooms. Serena watched him for a moment before turning back to the onion. They chopped vegetables in companionable silence for several minutes before she reached for the basket of eggs on her counter and began cracking them into a bowl.

"You don't keep them in the fridge?" Micah brought his pile of diced mushrooms over and set them next to her neat stacks of ingredients. It was a good, uniform dice.

"I bought them at Bigby Farm yesterday. Since they're not processed like commercial eggs are, they don't need any special treatment. That's some good knife work." Using a fork, she whipped the eggs into a frothy mixture.

"Interesting. We get most of our eggs locally for the bakery—we can't always get the quantity we need—but we keep them in the fridge. That doesn't matter, does it?"

"I don't see why it would." Serena set her omelet pan on the burner and turned on the gas. When it had warmed, she dropped in some butter. "What do you want? Little bit of everything?"

Micah nodded.

She scooped in toppings and stirred them around until the onions started to turn transparent. Serena's shoulders loosened as she went through the familiar movements of pouring the egg over the toppings and pushing them around in the pan so they were evenly distributed. "Could you look in the fridge for the cheese? There's a container—it's already shredded."

He came back with a sealed tub. "This?"

"That's the one." Serena slid her spatula around the edges of the omelet before giving the pan a little shake. Nodding at how easily the contents slipped around, she gave the pan a fast shove and flick that flipped the eggs expertly.

"I've only ever seen Jonah manage that. The few times I've tried, I end up eating scrambled eggs scraped up off the stovetop. Sometimes the floor."

She laughed and turned to meet his gaze. "It just takes practice. And a small pan. I don't try it with anything larger. You want cheese?"

"Yeah."

They both reached for the tub at the same time and their hands met. Electricity sparked up her arm. There'd been tingles at church but here, now, it was like a supernova. She drew back and let Micah peel open the lid. She reached in and sprinkled the grated cheese she'd found at the farmers market over the top before flipping half over and sliding Micah's eggs onto a plate. "Mine will just be a minute. I have everything else set out on the table in the dining room—it's through that door."

Micah pointed.

Serena nodded and started her toppings cooking. She'd bought some cinnamon swirl bread from their bakery stall at the market yesterday as well. Malachi had been the only one manning the booth, and it seemed he hadn't spilled the beans that she'd been by, searching for Micah more than bread. Still, the sweet bread would go well with omelets and fresh fruit. She flipped her eggs over and finished up her own lunch.

"This looks amazing. How'd you get so much done already?" Micah pulled out the chair at her place.

Heat crept across her cheeks. She set her plate down and sat, eyebrows lifting as he helped scoot her chair back in. "I chopped a lot of the toppings up before church. I just had to pull them out when I got here."

He grinned. "What if I'd said no? Or convinced you to go out?"

She shrugged. "It'd all keep well enough and I'd be set for the week. But I'm glad that's not how it ended up."

"Me too." He held out his hand, palm up. "Can we pray?"

Bracing herself, she put her hand in his. The jolt was less pronounced, but still there. She bowed her head and waited. He didn't want her to say the blessing, did he? Praying out loud was still considerably outside her comfort zone.

"Dear Jesus, thank you for this food. Please bless it to our bodies. Be with us as we spend time together, let our thoughts and deeds be honoring to You. Amen."

Micah squeezed her fingers before letting go and reaching for a slice of bread. "Is this from the bakery?"

"Yeah. I bought it from Malachi yesterday at the market." She cut the corner off her eggs. "I was hoping to run into you. Gloria said you usually worked there on Saturdays?"

"Usually. Jonah needed an extra hand in the kitchen, so we propped the door and kept an ear out for customers. Mal's...not an asset when it comes to the actual baking. But I'm sorry I missed you."

His words warmed her. Maybe she wasn't too forward, after all. "It worked out okay. I got to visit your church and meet the rest of your family. And you still came for lunch. All's well that ends well."

"I've always preferred *Much Ado About Nothing* or *Midsummer's Night Dream*, but that works."

She grinned and took another bite of eggs. "You like Shakespeare?"

"What's not to like? Drama, intrigue, comedy—even the romance isn't so over the top that it makes you gag."

Her eyebrows lifted. "Not into romance?"

His cheeks reddened, but he held her gaze. "Not in my reading material, no."

He'd emphasized reading material just enough to make her heart lift. He did feel it—he had to. "You're missing out. Romance is one of my favorite things."

When the food was gone and the dishes stacked in the dishwasher, Serena slipped her hand into Micah's and tugged him toward the patio doors. "Let's go for a walk. Unless you need to go?"

"I have time. Sunday is the one day of the week where I don't have any work or family obligations. And usually those are the same thing since I work with family."

"Do you like it? Working with your brothers? Living here in the same town as your sister? It's not too much, too close?" Some days L.A. had been stifling. Even in a big city, her parents had been everywhere—or people who knew her parents. And if it wasn't family, it was photographers and fans all trying to see whether she'd asked for extra whipped cream on her coffee and speculating about the tiniest bit of weight gain. In Arcadia Valley, since no one really knew who she was, they never looked too close.

"Most days. And when it feels like there's nowhere to get away, I go for a walk or take over deliveries and head into Twin Falls. A little change of pace just to mix things up is usually all I need. I thought I'd miss D.C., but I don't. Do you miss California?"

Serena led him around the back of her studio toward the river that flowed along the border of her property. "There's nothing for me there now."

"Your parents? Grandparents? Friends? Aren't they all still there?"

"They all expect me to be someone I can't be anymore." Serena gazed at the sunlight glinting off the surface of the water.

"What do you mean?" Micah gently squeezed her hand. There was no reason for the simple gesture to impart such strength. But it did.

"Derrick and I..." She paused and pressed a hand to her chest to soothe the ache before starting again. "Acting was all I knew for as long as I can remember. I was on set with my parents, or my grandparents, until they got me my first role. Then it became a circus of what time who had to be where and how we were all going to get where we needed to be. I liked it. I can't say I didn't. But there was always something missing, some part of me that felt empty. And then I met Derrick when I was seventeen and there was practically an audible click."

Micah's hold on her hand loosened. "You were off and on—more off than on, it seemed—for a number of years though."

She laughed. So he wasn't oblivious to who she was, after all. Why should that matter? Hadn't she convinced herself she wanted someone who had no idea about her past? Someone who could love her solely based on who she was today? Not that they were anywhere near love, but the point was the same...maybe it was better this way after all. "We were. I was young and doing anything I could to get my parents' attention. I wouldn't have admitted that then, mind you. That's the hindsight of time and therapy. Derrick was basically in the same boat. But neither of us could stay away—it wasn't the healthiest of relationships. The night of my twenty-first birthday we finally stopped playing games with each other and, after all the party guests were gone, we got in his little plane, flew to Vegas, and got married. He loved the plane—we took it out every chance we got."

"No one knew you were married." He pulled his hand away and tucked it in his pocket.

"No, they didn't. We didn't want to ruin it with the frenzy that would certainly happen. And we'd lived together off and on anyway." She winced. So much of her life had been lived in almost gleeful violation of how God wanted things done. Although, it was just the way things were—she hadn't known any different. Could Micah see past that? Would he be willing to forgive her past like Jesus had? "He'd been having seizures for about six months. They were random, unpredictable, and he refused to go to the doctor. I think I'd almost convinced him...but he never got the chance. We were flying out to Catalina Island for the weekend. He started to shake just as we were making our approach. That airstrip is at the top of the mountain, there's no room for error...everyone says it's a miracle..."

Micah turned and opened his arms. "I'm sorry."

Serena stepped into his embrace. She took a deep, shuddering breath as his arms wrapped around her. "I was in the hospital a long time. I was ejected through the window—I'd unhooked my seatbelt to try and help Derrick steady—my face...well, you've seen the scars. Derrick was gone on impact. But in the hospital, in the long hours of the night, I finally listened to God knocking on my heart's door. And I knew when I got out that I couldn't go back. My family keeps asking when I'm going to get over 'this Jesus thing'—that's what they call it, like it's a new diet I'm trying out and will give up eventually—and come home to carry on their legacy. But I can't."

His hands made gentle, soothing circles on her back.

Serena eased back and looked up to meet his gaze. She hadn't intended to dump all that on him. Eventually, sure. He deserved the full story. But even with Gloria she'd dribbled it out in bits and pieces, gauging her reactions. "Sorry. I—"

"Shh." Micah laid a finger over her lips. "I'm glad you told me."

His gaze flicked to her mouth then back to her eyes. Serena's heart galloped in her chest as his hands clenched at her waist. She drew in a breath to speak.

"Serena?"

There were so many questions in that one whispered word and only one response to all of them. Unable to speak, she nodded.

His grin flashed before he drew her close and lowered his lips to hers. Serena closed her eyes and leaned into him. Everywhere they touched was a tiny shower of sparks in her system. She slid her hands around his neck and wove her fingers through his hair. Maybe this wasn't what she'd planned when she'd suggested they walk down by the river, but she certainly wouldn't be complaining anytime soon.

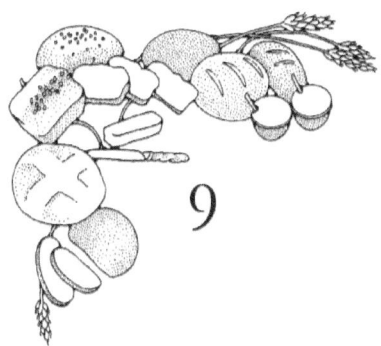

9

Micah whistled as he set the cookies and muffins in the display cases. The croissants Jonah finally deemed good enough to try filled three shelves. Malachi said to include four in each subscription order as they were picked up, but it still seemed like a lot for a new offering. On the other hand, they were filled with chocolate, and that was always a pretty easy up-sell.

"You're cheerful today." Jonah stacked another tray on the counter and crossed his arms. "I didn't realize you were that excited about the croissants."

Micah laughed. "You have to admit, they're really good. How'd you get the pastry so flaky?"

"I'll teach you. It's a pain, but it's worth it." Jonah strode to the coffee machine and filled a cup. "You're really not going to say?"

"Say what?" Micah avoided his brother's gaze and continued loading the display cases. He'd successfully avoided his family when he got home yesterday, but that wasn't surprising, everyone had things to do on Sunday afternoons, even if was just taking a nap. Still, he wasn't in a hurry to share the details of his time with Serena.

That kiss...well, there'd been more after the first one. He grinned. When would he see her again?

"That. You're grinning for no reason." Jonah sipped his coffee. "I take it lunch went well?"

Micah nodded. "She's a good cook."

"You ate at her place? I thought you were going out."

He shrugged. "We talked about it, but then she mentioned omelets, and that sounded like a good plan."

"Mmhmm. More private, too."

Heat crawled up his neck. "That too."

"Nice." Jonah gave Micah's shoulder a light punch. "I'm glad you got over yourself."

"What's that supposed to mean?" Micah brushed off his hands and slid the backs of the display cases closed.

"Your little meltdown about her being famous? Do you not remember that?"

He hadn't had a meltdown. He'd grown up hearing about all the men she'd had in her life—and back then, she'd gone through them like tissues during allergy season. Then there'd been Derrick King. Whom she'd married. That had been a shock. He rubbed the back of his neck. "Look. I have concerns—even still—that I think are valid. But I'm not going to say we can't explore a relationship until I have all my questions answered."

Jonah snorted. "If you want my advice..."

"Not really."

Jonah chuckled. "Too bad. Don't screw this up. She's good for you."

"You'd say that about any woman with a pulse who showed interest in me."

"Maybe. Doesn't mean it isn't true." Jonah pushed back through the door that took him to the kitchen.

Micah frowned. Was he that desperately in need of whatever it was having a girlfriend provided? He didn't wear stripes with plaid or navy blue and black at the same time. He had no trouble socializing with the customers who came to the bakery. Having an affinity for books—which Jonah shared—and quiet evenings at home didn't make him a social misfit.

Whatever.

The bell above the door chimed as the first pickup of the morning came in. He pushed his brother's concern away and smiled. Maybe Jonah was jealous. Wouldn't that be a hoot?

Fire and Brimstone was doing a brisk lunch business as usual. Serena waved from a two-person table in the far corner of the restaurant. Micah smiled and squeezed through the crowd toward her.

"Hi."

She stood and wrapped her arms around him before pressing her lips to his cheek. "I'm sorry I've been so busy this week, but I'm really glad you suggested this."

Micah held her close for a minute before lightly brushing her lips with his. "I've been trying to figure out when I could see you again since I got home on Sunday."

Serena laughed and eased out of his embrace to resume her seat. "Me, too. How're things at the bakery?"

"We're having one of our best weeks since we opened, according to Mal. Jonah finally got the puff pastry working the way he wanted, so he's had croissants every morning—some chocolate filled, others plain. We can't keep them past noon." Micah scanned the menu before pushing it away. "I think he's going to have to make them a staple. If they disappear, we're liable to have riots in the parking lot."

"Ooh. I need one. Any way I can talk you into boxing a couple up for me tomorrow before you open?" She batted her eyelashes.

"I can probably be persuaded." Micah reached for her hand. "Are you free Friday night?"

"I don't know...it took you until Wednesday to ask me. I might be all booked up."

He frowned, his gaze latching on to hers. She was teasing, right? "Oh. Well, maybe another time."

"Hey. I was joking."

He grinned. "Gotcha."

"Ding-a-ling." Serena shook her head and laughed.

The server appeared at their table. Micah briefly debated trying something new, but gave in and got what he always did. Serena ordered the same thing. "I don't know why I even look at the menu. I always think I'm going to branch out, and then I'm back to where I always am."

She nodded. "Same problem here. On the other hand, why mess with a good thing?"

"How's your work going?" He should know a better way to ask that, something that showed he paid attention when she talked. Which he did. But the terms she used floated around and never really took root in his brain, and he wasn't going to ask if she'd enjoyed her week of playing with clay.

"Really well. That big vase I made last week is shaping up nicely. I think it's going to be stunning, and I'm usually not positive until I get something out of the kiln. I threw a few special orders this morning and hope to glaze some others this afternoon. The plates for the bakery are drying nicely. I think they'll be ready to go into the kiln for the next fire, probably the middle of next week. The mug experiment didn't work like I'd hoped." Serena frowned. "Big bummer there. So I can either paint on the same basic design I did for the plates, or I can do something interesting with mocha diffusion. Have a preference?"

She'd explained mocha diffusion to him before. Briefly. His main takeaway was that it was responsible for the delicate ferny patterns that spread out like fractals on a lot of her work. "Either one will be fine. I can't imagine not liking anything you make."

Serena laughed. "Maybe I should ask your brothers then. I don't want them to think they got taken advantage of because we're dating."

Dating. The words warmed his insides. Even if it was surreal.

"What's surreal?"

Micah squeezed his eyes shut. "I said that out loud?"

She nodded, her eyes glinting with humor.

He cleared his throat. "Dating you. I...had a huge crush on you for basically all of my teenage years."

Her eyebrows lifted. "Yeah? How am I holding up?"

"Better than I imagined."

"Really?" Serena sipped her soda.

"Before you were just beautiful and talented."

She snorted. "*Alien Ninjas* did not showcase my talent."

He shrugged. "Depends on the audience, I'd say. Anyway. I just mostly liked to look. I'd read about your personal life, though, and all I could do was pray for you. Now you have Jesus, which kind of makes you perfect."

"I'm far from perfect." Serena studied their joined hands and her fingers tightened on his. "You really prayed for me?"

"Since I was fifteen."

Serena blinked rapidly, her eyes bright with unshed tears.

"Hey." Micah's throat went dry and his heart hammered in his chest. "I didn't mean to make you cry. It was supposed to be a good thing. Or at least maybe not a bad one. I shouldn't have said anything. I'm sorry."

"No. Don't be sorry. Don't ever be sorry for something like that. I needed someone to pray for me back then. I...should do better about praying for my friends in L.A. I'm not sure why it never occurred to me to do that." Serena dabbed at her eyes with her napkin.

He watched her before nodding slowly. "You okay?"

"I really am." She leaned back as the server appeared with their pizzas. "Thank you."

He squeezed her hand. "Can I pray with you, now?"

"I'd like that a lot."

Micah bowed his head and waited for his thoughts to settle before offering a short prayer of gratitude for the food and for Serena. There might be questions and doubts still lurking at the back of his mind, but for now, in this moment, he was going to focus on her and see where things went. Surely if God wanted them together, He'd make it clear.

Micah smoothed the front of his button-down shirt. Should he wear a sport coat, too, or was that too fancy? He'd hoped to go to L'Aubergine, but when he called on Wednesday after their lunch, the restaurant had said they were booked. Apparently they did more business than he realized. So he'd fallen back on El Corazon. It was a nicer atmosphere than some of the places in town. Plus, he didn't get out there for lunch very often, so it was a treat. The only other option would be to drive into Twin Falls. Maybe he should've done that, but the food here in town was arguably better than anywhere else. People in Arcadia Valley cared about their food, and it showed.

He grabbed the coat and headed downstairs. Mal would know if he should wear the thing or not. Was this what Jonah had meant when he'd said Micah needed a woman in his life?

"Whoa. Fancy." Mal waggled his eyebrows and set the controller for the game console aside. "And a bowtie. I thought you gave those up?"

Micah shrugged. "I don't really wear ties at all. But I thought this was kind of fun. Less stuffy than a regular tie. Is it too much?"

"No. It's cool. Did you get a reservation after all?"

Micah shook his head. "I figured we'd head to El Corazon instead. Seemed to work for you and Ursula."

Malachi grinned. "So it did. Even with the new menu, it's good food."

"The new menu's better than the old one. You might be the only person in town who doesn't agree with that statement. It's still good, solid Mexican food, but it's fresh. And local."

"Yeah, yeah. You should write their ad copy. Or ours." Malachi reached for the controller. "Even still, ditch the jacket. That's over the top."

Micah draped the coat over the back of the couch. "Noted. Hey, why aren't you on a date tonight?"

"Ursula, Ruth, and Pam are all in Twin Falls listening to some Christian women's speaker. I forget who. Anyway, it's tonight and all day tomorrow. Jonah and I dusted off the Vault Hunter CD. We haven't really spent much time doing that in a while. Emerson and Corban may stop by, but Emerson has the kids and Corban has to watch the B&B."

Huh. He would've enjoyed that. Not as much as going on a date with Serena, but still, they couldn't have asked him to join them? "The women's thing came up suddenly?"

"I think Pam got tickets a few months back. Why?"

"Just wondering why I didn't get an invite to the gaming fest."

"Our plans didn't get made until yesterday. We didn't figure you'd bail on Serena to play video games. Were we wrong?" Malachi cocked his head to one side.

"Nope."

"Didn't think so. Go. Have fun. You can play tomorrow."

"Okay. Later." Micah took a deep breath and headed for his car. Serena lived north of town. El Corazon was on the south end, closer to where he and his brothers lived in Corban's farmhouse. The smarter thing probably would've been to have her pick him up—she'd offered. But he just couldn't. So instead he'd be driving back and forth. At least the scenery was nice. He hadn't gotten over that in the year they'd been in town—so much different than the D.C. area on just about every level. It was better. Way better.

Before long, Micah pulled into Serena's driveway. Her house still made him pause. All the glass and wood inside and out...now, knowing who she was and the kind of money she had to have at her disposal, it made a little more sense. Had it been a custom build?

"Are you coming in?" Serena leaned over the railing of the deck and grinned. "Or should I just come out?"

"Sorry." Micah pushed away from the car and walked toward her. "I was admiring your house. Did you have it built when you moved here?"

She shook her head. "Would you believe the answer's no? The house is what sold me on Arcadia Valley. I had some work done before I moved in, and the studio's something I added. But the bones of the house were already here."

He gathered her in his arms and brushed his lips over hers. "You did a good job."

Serena blushed and stepped back, taking his hand in hers. "Come on in. I'm almost ready."

Micah followed and scanned the living room. "You've got some new pieces out."

"Yeah. I sold some of what had been in here, so I swapped in some new stuff. You like it?"

"I do." He picked up a shallow bowl that had curlicues of different colored clay spiraling across the surface. It made him think of the circus. He carefully set it back down and crossed to a tall vase he didn't recognize.

Serena smiled at him and disappeared down the hall that led, he assumed, to her bedroom.

One of these days, he'd like to see the rest of the house. From the public rooms he'd been in, he suspected he'd love it, but he wanted to know what all was included. And yet, asking for a tour might not be the best idea. He didn't need to put either of them in a situation where they'd be tempted to take things too far. Especially when she was no stranger to those sorts of activities. His stomach twisted. Best not to think about that.

"All set." She came back into the living room with a shawl draped over her arm and a tiny purse in her hand. The thing probably held her nothing more than her phone and a pen. Why even bother? The fitted navy blue dress hugged her curves in all the right places. His mouth went dry.

"You look great."

"Thanks. You're looking rather dapper yourself." Serena beamed and flicked his bowtie. "I'm not sure I realized these could be anything other than grandfatherly. But it's working for me."

Micah laughed and took her hand. "Come on. Let's go eat."

"I'm so excited. I haven't been to L'Aubergine as much as I'd like. Their food is amazing."

He winced as he pulled open the passenger door. "About that. They were booked. Is El Corazon okay?"

Serena blinked. "Sure. I love their food, too. But we're overdressed."

"I thought it might be fun, but if you want to change, you can. I can ditch the tie—"

"You know what? It's fine. You're right, it'll be fun. And I hear an enchilada with queso fresco calling my name."

Micah grinned and shut the door. He scooted around the car and slid into the driver's seat. "That's one of my favorites, too. Malachi was giving me a hard time about liking their new menu better, but really? How is garden-fresh not better?"

"That's one of the things I love about Arcadia Valley in general. Everyone seems to understand and appreciate good, fresh food." Serena shifted in her seat.

"How'd you end up here? It's a long way from California."

She let out a breath that was close to a sigh. "It took me a long time to heal after the accident. Once I was out of ICU and in a place where I was able to take a hard look at my life, I realized I didn't want everything to go back to the way it had been. For one thing, Derrick was gone..."

"We don't have to talk about it. I don't want to make you sad." Micah reached over and clasped her hand, giving himself a firm mental kick for having not thought through the whole topic of conversation in the first place.

"Long story short, we'd visited Twin Falls one weekend when Derrick was filming in Idaho and both of us loved it. I couldn't find exactly the right property there, though, when I started my house hunt. Finally, the woman I was working with sent me a link to the property I bought with about a hundred apologies for it not being exactly what I wanted. But I fell in love. It might not have been what I said I was looking for, but it was perfect."

He nodded and turned into the parking lot for El Corazon. If the number of cars was any indication, they were doing a brisk business this evening. "I'm glad that's how it worked out."

Serena grinned. "I am, too. And not just because it meant I got to meet you. So many people here in Arcadia Valley have changed me. Gloria, in particular. She took me under her wing right off the bat, dragged me kicking and screaming to church with her. And I can never repay her for helping me find Jesus. I started listening in the hospital, but I didn't really know what I was doing. Gloria connected those dots."

Micah nodded. He couldn't imagine what it would be like to have grown up without the quiet, steady influence of godly parents like he had. It was no wonder, really, that she'd lived the way she had if no one ever told her the right way. And yet, hadn't she noticed the emptiness? The few years in college when Micah had tried to go his own way, he'd been plagued by the void.

Inside the restaurant, Micah glanced around and smiled at the decor. The bright colors were happy and warm. And they made him hungry. Or maybe that was the mix of spicy scents that filled the air.

Despite the crowd, they were seated quickly and given a bowl of chips and salsa to enjoy while they perused the menus.

"I'm not even looking. There are too many tempting possibilities and I want those enchiladas." Serena reached for a chip and swirled it in the salsa.

"Did you hear the group of older women as we walked in?" Micah set his menu aside and snagged a chip. "They thought we looked good and wished more people took the time to dress up for an evening out."

Serena chuckled. "Well. I'm glad we made someone's night."

"I'm sorry I didn't let you know about L'Aubergine. We'll try again. Promise."

"That's a deal. Although, I like a picnic in the park just as well."

He smiled. "That's good to know. Speaking of parks, I thought after we ate we could take a stroll through Arcadia Creek Park."

"Sounds great." She reached across the table for his hand.

Micah wound his fingers through hers, still not quite able to wrap his mind around the fact that he was with her.

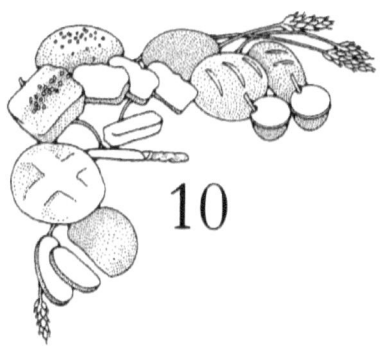

10

Serena idly reached for the phone as it began to ring, not taking her eyes off the spreadsheet on her computer monitor. She could afford to hire someone to handle this. Why didn't she? Right. She wanted to keep her hands in it.

"Hello?"

"Serena, girl, this script is amazing."

Serena frowned and dragged her thoughts away from the numbers. "Zennia?"

Her friend snorted. "You didn't check your caller ID again. Are you busy creating masterpieces out of blobs of clay? I can call you back—or just tell you I'm overnighting this script. You let me know when you're coming into town to do the reading. There's no question it was tailor-made for you."

Script? "I'm not...is this from Jerry?"

"Duh? He said you knew it was coming. Seemed a little put out that he couldn't deal with you directly, but he ought to know better. Even after five years, you're a hot commodity. I get six or seven calls a week with comeback offers."

"Seriously? You never say anything." Serena clicked open her email and typed her mother's address in. She'd been pretty clear that she wasn't interested. Hadn't she told her mother not to give Jerry the okay? And yet here she was, talking to Zennia about it.

"You told me you're not interested. I figure you'll let me know when that changes. And from what I've read of this script, you held out for the right part. It's epic."

Serena laughed. Epic. That was so Zennia. "I miss you. When can you come visit? It's been too long."

"We'll hang when you come out for the reading."

"Zennia, I'm not coming out for any readings. I asked my mother to tell Jerry no. Just send it back to him and let him know I'm not interested. Same as you do for any of the other people who are still trying to believe the lie that I have something to offer the acting world." Serena closed the email without typing anything. There was no point. Her mother was...her mother. She meant well. Or at least her mom *thought* she meant well. Her mother just refused to believe that she didn't have the right to decide what was best for Serena anymore.

"Nope. I'm sending this one on. And I'm making you promise me you'll read it. I know you roll your eyes when I say something's epic, but this one? It really is. This is the kind of script we were dreaming of five years ago."

"Zen—"

"What's it hurt to read it?"

Serena sighed. "Yeah, all right. I'll read it, but I'm not taking the part. I'm done with that—it's another life as far as I'm concerned."

"Still the Jesus thing? I keep waiting for you to outgrow that."

"It's not going to happen, Z. I wish you'd let me tell you about Him. Do you remember how miserable I was? All the pills I was on just to get through the day?"

"Sure, but Derrick got you through most of that."

Derrick had helped. He'd been a little ahead of her in terms of discovering Jesus—she had to believe he'd accepted Christ, although he'd never said as much to her. But something had changed in him—they'd gotten married because he convinced her they shouldn't sleep together again unless they did. He loved her and for the first time in her life, she believed someone meant it when they said the words. "Only by planting little seeds the whole time about his own newfound faith."

"Derrick?" Zennia made a rude noise. "What's the world coming to? Look, I'm not going to say you have to ditch all the Jesus stuff if you're determined to hold onto it, but read the script and schedule a reading. It's time for you to come back home. Oh, and that tall oval vase you posted in-process photos of? I want it. Soon's it done, you know where to send it."

Serena's eyebrows lifted. "I didn't realize you followed my pottery website."

"Yeah, well, I'm still trying to decide if I can sue you for breach of contract. I think, technically, you owe me a percentage from your sales." The laughter behind her friend's words made it clear she was joking.

"I'll just price the vase accordingly and make it a gift."

Zennia laughed. "This is why we need you back in town. Read the script and come home."

The line went dead. Serena set her phone down and shook her head, scooting back from her desk to look around.

She already was home.

Serena arranged the last shelf of the kiln and stepped back. The spacing looked fine and everything should have had ample time to dry. With a quick prayer, she closed the lid and set the temperature and timer.

"Hey there, stranger." Gloria strode into the studio in jeans and a T-shirt. "Haven't seen you in town this week. Or in a particular bakery...everything okay in paradise?"

Serena laughed. "It's good. I've just been busy, as has Micah. I think we're doing something tomorrow—picking peas and spinach at the community garden near his church or some such? I didn't pay a lot of attention once he said garden, honestly."

"The garden's a great project. The vegetables they produce are donated to Corinna's Cupboard—they feed the homeless." Gloria crossed her arms. "You don't look convinced."

Serena shrugged. "I don't like getting dirty."

Gloria pressed her lips together, clearly trying to hold in a laugh. "Right."

"Seriously. I don't. Why are you laughing?"

Gloria gave up trying to hold in her mirth and gestured to the studio as she chortled. "You're a potter. You work with mud. For a living."

Serena's lips twitched, but she crossed her arms. "It's different."

"How?"

"It just is. Clay—*not* mud—is different than dirt. It doesn't get under my fingernails, for one thing. And if it does, it washes out when I wash my hands, no scrubbing and weird brushes that still leave black gunk there for days. Plus, clay isn't itchy and filled with bugs." Serena shuddered. "But he's determined that it's going to be fun. Says his whole family's going. So, I guess I'm going to go pull weeds or whatever."

Gloria grinned. "Try not to sound so excited when you get there."

"You off tomorrow? You could come, too. Jonah's going to be there." Serena waggled her eyebrows.

"I might swing by. But you know we're just friends, right? I think I've told you this a thousand times." Gloria frowned. "You just bring it up to make me crazy."

"It's more that I don't understand." Serena swiped a sponge over her workspace and gestured toward the door. "He's handsome—you've admitted that—and you have good conversations. What's the problem?"

"I'm not looking for a man, is all. I have a job I love, but it's not one that lends itself to having marriage and a family. Even in a little town like Arcadia Valley." Gloria stepped out of the studio and waited while Serena checked that the door had locked.

Serena studied her friend as they crossed to the house and up the stairs to the deck. Jonah knew she was a cop and still flirted shamelessly with her, so he must not mind her career choice. Of course, he could be one of those guys who was fine with your job until it started impeding his ability to have you do stuff for him, but it didn't seem likely. The Baxter brothers—all three of them—seemed to have their heads on straight. Look at Micah—he knew all about her Hollywood days and yet, for some reason, seemed content to date her now that she was just a potter. None of that was worth bringing up to Gloria though. Her friend's face was set in its unmovable force look. That was probably why she was such a good cop. "Some of the people on the force are married. With families and everything. Aren't they?"

Gloria huffed out a breath. "Fine. Maybe it works for some people. I just don't think I'm one of them. It's not like I spend my off hours dreaming of cooking, cleaning, and doing laundry while birds tweet in circles around me. I'm not princess material."

"Who needs a princess? I don't get the feeling that's what Jonah wants at all. You're friends, you flirt...that's a good place to start, isn't it?"

"Yeah, I guess. If I was looking. I just don't think romance is what God has for me, no matter how much I might want it. What are we up to tonight?"

Probably no point in pushing any further. Not if she wanted Gloria to stay for the evening like they'd planned. "Movie or board game? Your choice."

"Movie. Definitely. I get to pick. You have terrible taste in movies."

"And yet, we're choosing from what I own. So, I'm not sure how getting to choose helps you." Serena squatted by the cabinet that held her DVD collection and pulled open the doors. "Knock yourself out, though."

"Are we eating? 'Cause I could eat." Gloria plopped down in front of the movies and angled her head to read titles.

"I have pork chops I can grill and then throw together a salad, or we can order pizza. Have a preference?"

"If you don't mind grilling, I'm all about not fast food. My shift was weird so many times this week that I ate more than my fair share of takeout." Gloria gave a mock shudder and pulled a DVD case from the shelf, setting it down on the floor beside her.

"Sure. Found a movie already?" Serena took the chops out of the fridge and eyed them. She'd planned to marinate them, but never got around to it. With a shrug, she got out a bottle of barbecue sauce and squirted a dollop on each one before smearing it over both sides. That'd do. She washed her hands before grabbing the plate and crossing to the deck. "I'll go get these started."

"'K. I'm still considering options." Gloria added another movie to the growing stack by her leg.

Laughing, Serena stepped out onto the deck and set the plate with the pork chops down on the small deck table. She tugged the cover off her grill and checked that the gas was turned on. Every now and then she thought about switching to charcoal—no one could argue the taste wasn't better—but it was so much more work and time, and when she grilled, it was usually spur of the moment, like this. She turned the dial to ignite and pressed the switch, smiling as the gas came on with a whoosh, and closed the lid. It'd heat up in no time.

A white package truck lumbered into her driveway. She waved at the driver and skipped down the steps to meet him.

"Hope I didn't keep you waiting, it's been a long day." The driver grinned and scanned the thick envelope before offering it to her.

"Nope. It's no rush. Thanks." Serena accepted the package and fought a shiver of anticipation. It was just a script. One she didn't even want, at that. Yet there was still that hidden thrill in her heart. Just possibilities and the unknown. She liked her life here and wasn't heading back to L.A. anytime soon. "Have a good one."

The driver beeped his horn as he navigated a three-point turn to get his truck turned around and facing the right direction.

Serena tossed the package through the open door on the deck toward the couch. It landed on the floor and slid partially under. She shrugged. Close enough. And the grill was ready. She flipped the lid back open and laid the chops on the metal grate before turning the knob to lower the heat slightly. Satisfied, she lowered the lid and carried the plate back inside.

"Okay. We're down to these four." Gloria held up the DVD boxes. "Any particular favorites?"

"Not this one." Serena tapped a romance filled with tragedy. "I'm not in the mood to sob uncontrollably tonight."

Gloria laughed. "Even when you know how it ends?"

Serena shrugged. "Any of the other three are fine by me. Flip a coin if you need to."

Gloria frowned at the three contenders before taking one and setting it on the coffee table. "What's the package?"

"Just something from my agent."

Gloria dropped the other DVDs and reached for the envelope. "It's thick. Heavy. Like a contract, I imagine. Or a script?"

Serena set the plate in the sink and washed her hands again without turning. She moved to the fridge and gathered salad ingredients. When she turned, Gloria was right there with the package in her hands, grinning.

"It's a script, isn't it? Are you going back to acting?"

Serena stepped around her friend and set her armful on the counter. "Yes, it's a script. No, I'm not going back to acting. My mom told the guy to send it to my agent, who nagged me into promising to read it. So I'll read it and then I'll decline. I'm happy here."

"But you were so good in the movies you did. Sure, *Alien Ninjas* wasn't amazing, but the rest...I've never understood how you could just walk away completely." Gloria hugged the script to her chest. "Couldn't you do a little and just come back here between movies?"

That...was an interesting possibility. There were a few people who managed to have a normal life away from L.A. Could she be one? She shook her head. "I don't know. Everyone back there expects me to be a certain way. To live a particular kind of life."

"That was five years ago. Surely they wouldn't expect you to still be who you were when you were barely twenty-one?"

Serena looked out the glass doors that led to the deck. Smoke billowed from the grill. "Make a salad, would you? I need to check the chops."

She grabbed tongs from the jar on her counter and hurried outside. Flipping up the lid, she let out a breath. Not burned. The smoke was just from the fat and sauce dripping. She flipped the chops. They were nearly ready. She might as well wait here. After another couple of minutes, she turned the knob to shut off the gas and stacked one pork chop on top of the other so she could grab both with the tongs.

"Can you get out a plate?" Serena strode quickly through the living room with the meat. She didn't want to drop it or drip.

Gloria set a plate on the counter. "You didn't answer my question."

"I'm not sure I have an answer. It's something to think about, anyway. Besides, the script could be terrible."

Gloria laughed. "Like that'd stop anyone in Hollywood from making the movie."

Serena shook her head and got down a second plate. "You have a point. Are we eating at the table or in front of the movie?"

"Let's get the movie started. Then maybe we have time for a double feature."

Serena's eyebrows lifted. It was rare for Gloria to want to stay longer than a quick meal or a movie. To even consider two? Something had to be going on. Hopefully, she'd be able to pry it out of her friend before the night was over.

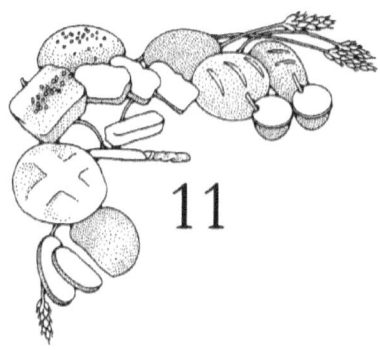

11

"You're gardening in that?" Micah glanced down at his faded jeans and old T-shirt then back at the form-fitting dark-wash jeans and designer T-shirt Serena wore. "I mean, you look amazing, but you know we're going to get dirty. Right?"

Serena sighed. "Yes, I know. But I can't wear my potting clothes out in public. I just can't. These wash."

He shrugged. It wasn't a big deal to him, either way, but she was probably going to be annoyed if she ended up grubby. She'd worn work clothes to the bakery when she wanted to show off her design for the plates. Apparently that was a different situation. "Okay. You ready?"

"Yeah. I know you think it's stupid."

"No. I don't. Maybe I don't understand, but I don't think it's stupid. As long as you know you're going to get dirt all over you, and are good with it, then I'm set." He held out his hand.

She wound her fingers through his and tugged, pulling him to her. She lifted her face and pressed her lips to his. "Or we could stay here and find something else to do."

"Um." Micah's heart raced off like someone had fired a starting pistol.

"That came out wrong." Serena stepped back, her cheeks pink. She cleared her throat. "So we should go ahead and go."

He nodded. His throat was dry. And the pictures that flashed through his mind—a combination of his vivid imagination and photos that had been included in online reports about her wild days—were definitely not where his thoughts should be. "That's a good plan."

In the car, Micah glanced over. "Have fun with Gloria last night?"

"I really did. It's rare for her to get a Friday night off and not be too tired to hang out. Thanks for understanding."

"My brothers appreciated a chance to trounce me at their latest video game—so that was fun."

Serena laughed. "What game?"

"No clue. There were zombies in a beach resort. I thought we were all fighting together to find a cure or something, but they managed to turn it into a competition to see who could slay the most of each type." He shook his head. "Still fun, though."

"Sounds like it."

"Ha. I hear your skepticism. And that's okay. It's not for everyone. I bailed around nine anyway so I could read. Managed to finish the thriller I picked up for free the other day."

"Yeah? How was it?"

"Eh. Not terrible, but not the best I've ever read." Micah grinned. "But I can't complain about the price, so I won't say anything bad about it. Do you like to read?"

"Sure. Maybe not as much as you, but I get through around twenty books a year. Maybe a few more. I'm more of a romance gal."

"Figures. Talk to Ruth sometime, she'll hook you up. She has this major thing for Christian romance—lots of authors to choose from." He turned into the parking lot at the church. "I thought we'd park here and walk over. I'm not sure what the parking's like over there on a Saturday."

"That works. I'm glad we're getting a chance to hang out this week. I missed you."

Warmth spread through him and he turned in his seat, trailing a finger down her cheek. "I missed you, too. I wasn't going to say anything in case you thought it was weird."

She grinned. "Why would I think it's weird?"

He shrugged and pushed open his door. Didn't girls—women—not want a guy who was clingy? And missing someone when you'd been dating for less than a month definitely qualified. But if she didn't mind, he wasn't going to explain why she should.

"Which way?" Serena squeezed his hand.

Would he ever get used to the effects of her touch? He hoped not. He gave a little tug and started down the block. "It's just over here, about two blocks."

It was a quick walk to the community garden. There were already several groups of people working at a variety of tasks. Micah looked for his sister and Corban. They had to be here somewhere. They'd left before he'd headed up to get Serena. Malachi and Jonah were manning the bakery, so probably wouldn't make it. They should talk about closing on Saturdays. They did well enough during the week they could handle a full weekend off. Or at least closing at noon. Something to keep them all from burning out before another year passed. Right now they had a system that mostly allowed people time off when they needed it, but once Malachi was married and with it looking like Jonah and Gloria would end up together in a heartbeat as soon as they got past whatever was holding them apart...well, wives and families took time away from a business, which is just what they should do.

"Micah! There you are." Ruth dropped a handful of something—weeds?—onto a pile and hurried over. "Serena, I'm so glad you came. This is going to be so much fun. We're down here in this bed weeding. They're going to compost everything, so we're making a big heap and we'll haul it over to where they're set up for composting later."

"Sounds good." Micah followed his sister, tugging on Serena's hand to get her moving along. "They have a picture of what the weeds look like? Knowing me, I'm going to pull up a plant they wanted."

Serena chuckled. "I'm sure you'll be fine."

Ruth grinned. "You're a riot, Micah. Here. Get weeding."

Micah knelt by the side of the garden bed and considered. The weeds were pretty obvious. That was good. He hadn't been joking. It'd been a while since he'd had to pull weeds in his mother's garden, and he'd never been particularly adept at growing things on his own. No matter how much he tried.

Serena settled beside him and flicked the leaf of a plant. "So, what are we pulling?"

"And you laughed at me? Here this kind," he pointed to one, "and these. If you focus on those, we should be fine."

"All right." Working her hand to the bottom of the weed, without actually touching the dirt, she yanked.

"You have to put some muscle behind it." Micah leaned over and kissed her cheek before he covered her hand with his own and nudged her fingers down to where the weed came out of the ground. "Now pull."

She did. The weed came free, trailing long roots with it. Serena grinned. "I did it!"

"So you did. Now do another." He winked and reached for his own to pull. Had she never weeded a garden before? The glee on her face when each plant came free was hard to look away from. He'd had so many doubts about this as a date—maybe it was going to work out after all.

Serena dropped another weed on her steadily growing pile, still grinning. "This is fun. Is that guy down there from the paper?"

Micah looked up and squinted. There was a tall guy with a camera moving around taking photos of their planting bed. "Dunno. I can't think why they'd be here. It's not an official work day or anything. There's just always some kind of labor needed, so the organizers have put the word out to the town that if people want to come and pitch in, they should do it. Who knows?"

Serena frowned and returned to her weeding.

Ruth came over with a basket. "Hey. I found these over in one of the greenhouses. You can put your weeds in it, makes it a little easier to haul them over to be composted."

"Where's that?" Micah scooped the weeds they'd already pulled into the basket and shielded his eyes with his hand.

Ruth pointed.

"I'll take these over and empty it and be back. 'K?"

"Sure." Serena smiled and tossed one more into the basket.

Micah walked past the man with the camera on his way to the compost pile. He didn't look familiar. Which didn't mean anything. Arcadia Valley wasn't so small that you recognized every face you walked past. And yet...he didn't fit. There was something about him that didn't seem local.

On his way back, he stopped and tapped the guy on the shoulder. "Hi there. You here to help?"

The man blinked and lowered his camera. "Oh. No. Just taking some pictures."

"For the paper?"

"If I can sell them. We'll see." He raised the camera again, twisted the lens, and clicked the shutter.

Sell them? "You're freelancing? Seems like that'd be hard in a little place like this. Do you do weddings and such as well to make ends meet?"

"Not really." He lowered the camera again. "Who are you?"

Micah's eyebrows shot up, but he brushed off his hand before extending it. "Micah Baxter. My brothers and I run A Slice of Heaven, the local community-supported bakery."

"Yeah? Local boy?" The man took his hand.

"Not really. We moved here about a year ago. You local?"

The man just smiled. "I'll let you get back to your weeding."

Weird. The dude was definitely odd. Micah nodded and strode back toward Serena. He scanned the beds for Ruth and Corban. They'd moved to the next bed over. He detoured and tapped Corban on the shoulder.

"Hey man, what's up?" Corban sat back on his haunches and looked up.

Micah squatted next to his brother-in-law. "You're local. You know that guy down at the end of the bed? With the camera?"

Corban leaned forward and looked, frowning. "Doesn't look familiar. I think I'd probably recognize the face if he was from around here. Could be up from Twin Falls though. Their paper's been running a series on gardening and farming in the area. Maybe they heard about this project?"

Micah shook his head. "Not the vibe I got. He said he'd be trying to sell his photos. Sounds more like a freelancer?"

"No clue. Why's it matter?"

Micah shrugged. "Probably doesn't. Just feels off. Thanks."

"If I hear anything, I'll let you know."

With a nod, Micah crossed back to Serena and knelt beside her. He kissed her cheek and loaded the small pile she'd created in his absence into the basket. "Did I miss anything?"

"Nope. What'd the guy say?" She leaned across some plants to grab a weed.

"Nothing useful. Some kind of freelancer, I guess." He shrugged and went back to weeding. "I can't imagine any circumstance where pictures of people weeding a community garden are going to be worth his time, but whatever. I'm not a photographer."

Serena looked up, her face pale. "He said that? A freelancer?"

"Yeah. Why?"

She shook her head, but she turned and stared at the end of the garden bed for several seconds. "Probably nothing."

"Sure? I can go talk to him again if you want?" Micah covered her hand with his. "You look like you saw a ghost."

"It's nothing." She smiled at him, but it didn't reach her eyes. "Let's get these weeds. It's more fun than I thought it'd be. I might come down here when I have some free time and do more. I don't need a reservation or anything, right?"

Micah laughed. "Nope. No reservations required."

Serena nodded and turned her focus to the weeds.

Micah frowned, watching her. There was something going on, but it was clear that she wasn't going to tell him right now. Which meant he should do what his girlfriend was doing and get to the gardening.

"Where's Serena?" Malachi signed the question as the worship band started the first song.

Micah shrugged. It was the same question he'd had since he'd called her that morning to see if he could pick her up for church and she hadn't answered. He signed back to his brother, "Maybe she changed her mind and went back to Arcadia Valley Community? I'll call her again after the service."

Malachi nodded, but his lips turned down in a frown.

Micah cast a glance over his shoulder, scanning the congregation. When he'd left her house after dinner last night, she'd said she'd see him here in the morning. So where was she? His gaze landed on the man from the garden yesterday. Why was he here?

He nudged Malachi's ribs and signed. "Remember the photographer I told you about?"

Malachi nodded.

"He's here."

Malachi's eyebrows lifted. "So he's going to church while he's on assignment. So what?"

His brother had a point. It was possible. Plausible, even. He'd been known to find a church to visit when he went on vacation. It didn't sit right. Serena's face when she'd looked at the guy. She'd tried to play it off, and he'd prodded a little, but she'd insisted it was nothing. So he'd let it drop.

Maybe that had been a mistake.

He cast one more glance over his shoulder as they sat for the sermon. It was hard to focus, but he wasn't going to look again. His phone vibrated. He switched out of the Bible app to check the text from Serena. It wasn't very informative—she'd overslept and wasn't feeling hot. She said she'd call him the next day.

He wanted to push, to tell her the guy was at church. Maybe ask about bringing her some soup or crackers if she was sick. But maybe they weren't there yet in their relationship. Even if he wanted to be. Micah tapped out a quick text letting her know he'd be praying for her and asked if there was anything he could do before switching back to the Bible passage.

After the benediction, Ruth scooted down the row to Micah. "Where's Serena? I thought she was coming today."

He shrugged. "She texted and said she wasn't feeling well."

Ruth frowned. "Does she need anything?"

"She said no. You wanna read her text for yourself?" He held out his phone.

"No. It's fine. I'm just surprised. And maybe a little disappointed." Ruth blew out a breath. "I was hoping she'd come for lunch."

"Yeah, me too." Micah lifted a shoulder. "But I guess I'm free, if there's still a spot at your table."

Ruth punched his arm. "Always. I think everyone's going to be there."

Micah forced a smile. Goody. There was nothing better than hanging out with newlyweds, soon-to-be-marrieds, and Jonah. That was unfair. He loved them—but right now he'd rather spend time with Serena. Still, it beat cooking. "I'll see you at the B&B."

"Can I catch a ride?" Malachi glanced over at Jonah. "He's heading back to the farmhouse first. I don't want to miss out on the food."

"Oh, please. I'm not going to take that long." Jonah shook his head. "See you in a bit."

Micah jerked his head toward the exit. "Let's go. Did you see which way that guy went?"

Malachi shook his head.

Bummer. Maybe he'd slipped out during the service. Micah needed to let it go.

Before long, they were seated around the table in the dining room at the bed and breakfast his sister, Ruth, and her new husband ran. Her guest rooms were full, but the people were all out for the day doing whatever it was people did when they vacationed in Arcadia Valley. It wasn't that there wasn't a lot to do and see—Idaho was an outdoorsman's paradise—but it wasn't the place Micah would choose for a getaway. Then again, camping had never been high on his list of things he wanted to do, and outdoorsy stuff was a close second on that same sheet of paper.

"This looks amazing, Ruth. Thanks." Jonah grabbed the bowl of mashed potatoes when Corban finished blessing their food. He turned to Ursula. "You need to swing by sometime and tell me your thoughts on the cakes. That way I know when I need to start and so forth."

Ursula grinned. "I can do that. Or you can look at my corkboard online."

Jonah shook his head. "If you want to print something off, you can do that. But I'm not hanging out on some female social media site."

"Guys use it too, you know. In fact, there are some great bread recipe boards. You might get ideas." Ruth reached for the salad. "I grab a lot of recipes from there."

"I think we'll manage. But thanks. Can you come this week? Usually I'm mostly done with the baking by noon." Jonah slid the potatoes to his left and took the platter of roast from Micah.

"Sure. I'll check my schedule and let you know. Or Mal can let you know. Either way."

Jonah nodded.

Ruth took a drink from her glass of water. "So. Speaking of wedding cakes."

Micah grimaced and stared at his plate. His sister had weddings on the brain.

"Jonah, I was wondering when you were going to ask Gloria out. Then everyone would be paired up." Ruth beamed at her brother before taking a bite.

Jonah shook his head.

"It's a fair question, man." Micah grinned. At least the conversation wasn't focused on him and Serena. Yet.

Malachi signed his agreement.

"For what it's worth—and I realize my vote might not matter yet—I like Gloria a lot." Ursula smiled.

"Look. I already asked her out. She said no. In very clear terms. She's not interested in anything more than being friends. Ever." Jonah stood, his chair clattering to the floor. "So could you just leave it alone?"

Ruth paled and half stood. "Please sit down. I'm sorry. I just thought..."

"It's fine." Jonah picked up his chair and sat. "But it wouldn't be wrong for people in this family to learn to mind their own business."

"They love you." Ursula cleared her throat. "That's something I noticed right away—you're a family who loves loudly, and you're all-in. So sure, maybe you get in each other's business, but no one can possibly say it's done for any reason other than love."

Jonah sighed.

"She's not wrong." Ruth smiled at Ursula. "So if not Gloria, what about Kenia at the bookstore? Or there's that nice—"

"Stop." Jonah shook his head. "Kenia's nice. And she's certainly pretty, but I'm beginning to think maybe God's calling me to be single. And, I can learn to be okay with that."

Micah blinked. Of the four of them, Jonah was the least likely to stay single—or at least that's what he would've said until two seconds ago. Honestly, he'd half-expected to be the solo uncle for the massive numbers of kids that Malachi, Ruth, and Jonah produced. It was one of the reasons he'd planned to always work with children in some capacity. But Jonah? He hadn't been single for more than a month at a time since he started dating in high school. At least not until they'd moved Arcadia Valley. And even with that, Jonah had been flirting with Gloria almost from day one.

"Don't make any hasty decisions." Malachi frowned across the table at Jonah. "Just be open to what God has for you, okay?"

Jonah shrugged. "Can we move on? I was hoping we'd get some more chances to give Micah a hard time about his movie star girlfriend."

Heat flooded Micah's face. "Former movie star."

Corban snorted. "Like that makes a difference. Aren't you worried one day she's going to wake up and realize she's way out of your league?"

Micah closed his eyes. "Constantly."

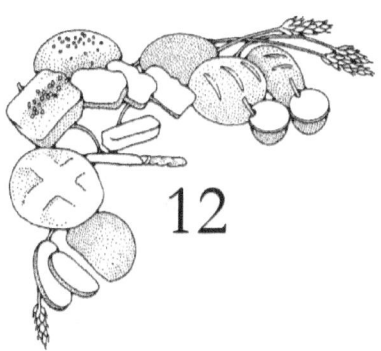

12

Serena checked the time as she paced the living room. Just after one. That made it noon in L.A. Close enough. Zennia should be up by now. She grabbed her phone and dialed.

"Mrph. Whozit?"

She couldn't stop the smile. "It's me. Sorry I woke you, although it *is* noon."

"Serena?" Muffled sounds whispered across the line. "Okay. Now I can talk. You read the script already? It's amazing, isn't it?"

Serena's gaze flicked to the script where it lay on her coffee table untouched. "Haven't even opened the envelope. I want to know what you did."

"I sent you a script. Like we talked about. What's going on?"

Did she really not know? "When you say you sent it...was it you, or did you have one of your assistants do it?"

A heavy sigh sounded in her ear. "I...don't remember. I probably...oh. No, I do remember. One of the girls was running down to the mail drop and we were getting close on time if I wanted it to get out like I promised, so I had her take it to the box. Why?"

"Do you trust her?"

"From the question, I'm gathering my answer needs to change to no. Will you *please* tell me what happened?"

Serena raked her fingers through her hair and sat, curling her legs under her. "I was spending some time with friends yesterday working in the community garden, and who should show up with his camera but Manzini?"

"Ohhhh...you're sure?"

"Really, Z? How many run-ins have I had with this guy? I'm sure. All he did, so far, was take pictures. He spun some story about being a freelancer to Micah, but that just clinched it."

"Micah? Hmmm. I must have missed your email telling me all about your new boyfriend. Let's stick a pin in that, shall we?"

Serena cringed. She hadn't meant to let that slip out. "Let's not. Do you think this assistant would've tipped Manzini off? I know he's been hounding my parents—and my grandparents for that matter."

Zennia snorted. "I'm surprised your mom managed not to say anything."

"Yeah, well, I threatened to cut her completely out of my life if she did. Since I actually followed through and moved to Idaho, she knows I will if she pushes it. If my family was going to sic the paparazzi on me, they would've done it before now."

"Would they?"

"Z."

"Hear me out. You didn't have a script—an amazing one, by the way—before. If you're poised for a comeback, some shots of you in your new native surroundings are just the right thing to get people primed for your return. Honestly, if I didn't know you better, I'd think you called him yourself."

Serena let her head fall back and stared at the ceiling. It was the kind of thing she might have done, once upon a time. But those times were long gone. She didn't want a comeback. She was only reading the script because she'd promised. "So, your admin?"

"Yeah, it's possible. She's new-ish and is supposed to mostly work for the other agents, but she helps Marci out now and then. Marci was sick, so...it was a perfect opportunity. I'll check into it." Zennia sighed. "Don't let this put you off that script."

"I said I'd read it." Serena reached for the envelope. She pulled the strip to open it and slid the script out. "See? Now it's open. I'll look at it this afternoon."

"Don't look at it. Read it. I'm serious. That part is amazing."

"Yeah, okay. Let me know if you find anything out. If it wasn't in your office, then I have to have a conversation with my mom that I'd rather not."

Zennia chuckled. "That's basically every conversation, isn't it?"

"Close." Her mother made it hard to keep her commitment to live like Jesus. Especially that love one another thing. "Sorry to bother you."

"Oh, no. Picture me pulling the pin out of a topic named Micah. Spill."

"Micah can be a girl's name, you know."

"Uh huh. Is Micah a girl?"

Serena groaned. She really didn't want to get into this with Zennia. The woman was relentless. And she loved gossip. She wouldn't *mean* to tell the world, but it would inevitably get shared. Not that she was liable to be able to keep a lid on things once those pictures got published. Not with the way Micah had brushed her hand and—had he kissed her cheek? She didn't remember. Regardless, there'd been some PDA. Most likely it had been caught on camera. "No. He's a baker. He and his brothers run a community supported bakery here in town. They catered my last kiln opening. The one you said you were going to try and get to?"

"Don't try to change the subject. I let you know I couldn't make it. And are you just friends?"

"I'd say we've moved past that."

"It's like pulling teeth. Details. Give me details."

Serena had never been so reluctant to share with her friend before. Not even about Derrick. Was it just that she'd grown used to privacy? "There's not a lot to share. He's fun to talk to. He always has something interesting to say. And he's challenging. He's been a believer longer than me, so he has insight that I don't."

"Ugly, then?"

She laughed. "No, Z, he's not ugly. I don't think even you could find a reason to object to me being seen with him."

"That hot? Really?"

"Really." Even if it wasn't her number one priority anymore, she couldn't discount it. "I like him. A lot."

"And him? Is it mutual?"

"Seems to be. His protective instinct came out with Manzini. I'm not sure how he'll react when I tell him who it was. He's...not from L.A. He hasn't spent his life around these kinds of people. He likes his quiet life here in Arcadia Valley." So did she, for that matter. And getting tracked down by photographers wasn't how she wanted her life here to be.

"Can't wait to meet him."

"Right."

"Please. You'll need someone to go to the premier with you."

"I said I'd read it, Z. I didn't say anything about taking the part. Lining up dates for the red carpet is just a tiny bit premature."

"Yeah, well, don't write it off 'til you've read the thing. Call me when you finish, no matter the time. Later."

Serena ended the call and shook her head. She should phone Micah and explain. She swallowed and tried to imagine how that conversation would go.

Or...she looked at the script and picked it up. She'd read a few pages and call later. A few hours one way or the other wasn't going to make a difference.

Serena stretched and looked around. It was getting dark. What time was it? She set the script on the coffee table, reached for her cell, and winced. Nearly seven. And there were a number of texts waiting for her. Her stomach growled. First things first—food.

She made her way to the kitchen, pausing to try and work the stiffness out of her limbs. That script...she sighed. What was she supposed to do now? She dug a chunk of cheese out of the fridge and pulled a loaf of bread from Micah's bakery out of the bag on the counter. She had a couple of cookies he'd made, too. She pursed her lips before adding them to her stack. Grabbing a plate from the cabinet, she dropped the food on it and carried her phone to the dining room table.

She didn't often bother eating at the table when she was alone. That was what the stools at the island were for. But it seemed like a change of position was in order. And it reminded her of the meal she'd shared with Micah, which in turn reminded her of their first kiss. A dreamy sigh escaped and she smiled before checking her texts.

They were all from Micah, making sure she was okay.

She drummed her fingers on the table before tapping Gloria's number.

"Hey there. Feeling any better?"

Serena's eyebrows shot up. "How'd you know I wasn't feeling well today?"

"Word gets around. I had to swing by Ruth's place to drop off a book I borrowed. She mentioned it. As did Micah. I take it you're better?"

"Yeah. I wasn't so much physically ill as disturbed. Did anyone mention the guy taking pictures at our garden workday yesterday?" She broke off a chunk of the aged cheddar and popped it in her mouth.

"Nope. What about him?"

In between bites of bread and cheese, Serena filled Gloria in. "I didn't want to run into him again today. And knowing him, he's lurking around town hoping for some kind of dirt."

"Did you tell Micah?"

"Not yet. I was sort of hoping I wouldn't have to."

Gloria snorted. "Oh, sure. Like you're going to get out of that. You need to tell him before he figures it out. 'Cause once he does, he's going to know you knew."

Serena sighed. Gloria had a point. Unfortunately. "While we're tangentially on the subject of my acting career...am I crazy for considering this part?"

"You read the script?"

"This afternoon. It's incredible. I figured it'd be more of the same and easy to pass up. But, Gloria, I don't know how to say no to this." Serena pinched the bridge of her nose as a dull ache started behind her eyes. "This is so not in my plans."

"Maybe not. But have you considered that it might be in God's?"

Pray about it. That's what she was saying. It was good advice. She still hadn't mastered the habit of taking things to God when she needed to make decisions. She weighed them against the Bible—obviously she wasn't going to do something that was sinful, not on purpose, at least—but the idea that He cared about the day-to-day decisions of her life was still hard to fathom. "No. Why would God want me back in that cesspit?"

"To shine a light?" Gloria cleared her throat. "Consider just for a minute the witness you could have. Especially with your history."

She closed her eyes. Or she could royally mess it up. "What if I'm not strong enough?"

"I think you underestimate yourself—and God—but I'll pray for you to have clarity."

"Thanks."

"I probably already know the answer, but I'm going to ask anyway. Have you talked to Micah about it?"

Serena sighed. "No. Not yet. I just read the script. What if he hates the idea?"

"Are you two serious enough that it matters?"

"I'd like to be. Does that count?"

"Totally." Serena could hear the grin in Gloria's voice. "He's a good guy. And I can't see him having a problem with it. But you won't know until you ask."

"Yeah, all right. Thanks."

"Anytime. I'm hanging up. You call Micah."

Serena ended the call and set the phone down. She broke a cookie in half and nibbled the edge. Micah had pointed out the house where he and his brothers lived when they'd driven to El Corazon. This seemed like a conversation that should be had in person. Maybe it was time for a Sunday evening drive.

Serena parked her car behind Micah's and turned off the engine. The farmhouse was exactly what it should be—white clapboard siding, a porch with rockers, and a big dog flopped on it. The little grassy space by the driveway held a gorgeous old tree that offered shade to two picnic tables. All it was missing was a tire swing and a big tin watering can. They probably had the can around here somewhere.

Her stomach clenched. Telling him before he found out was the right thing to do. So why was her heart racing? Her prayers were jumbled, words tumbling over one another in her mind. God knew what she meant—what she needed. She didn't even know if she'd get the part. Or if He even wanted her to try for it, although that seemed possible. Scripts like this didn't fall into her lap every day.

She watched as the screen swung open and Micah stepped out onto the porch. He squatted and ruffled the dog's ears. The dog responded by rolling onto his back. Serena smiled.

Micah looked up and their eyes met. Electricity sizzled between them. She took a deep breath. How was it possible to have something this potent between them in such a short period of time? Was it just lust? No. She pushed that thought away. What they had wasn't purely physical attraction. They were friends, had common interests. It was way more than simple chemistry.

Micah crossed the yard and knocked on her window.

Serena pushed the door open.

"You going to sit out here all night, or would you like to come in?"

She grinned, her muscles loosening. "It's a nice evening. I thought maybe we could go for a walk? I...we need to talk."

The blood drained from his face and his expression turned neutral. "Okay."

"It's not bad." Serena touched his arm as she got out and slid her keys into the pocket of her shorts. "At least I hope it isn't. I don't think it is."

His eyebrows lifted.

She blew out a breath. "Let's try that walk. Maybe I can untangle my tongue."

He smiled and patted his leg. The dog stood, stretched, and loped down the stairs from the porch to join them. "This is Spock. Spock, meet Serena."

The dog's butt plopped to the ground and he lifted a paw.

Serena laughed and leaned over, taking his paw in her hand. "It's nice to meet you. You're a good boy, aren't you?"

"He's Corban's. But he doesn't seem to care for it at the bed and breakfast, so he mostly hangs out here with us, though he'll wander over there now and then." Micah grabbed her hand and started to walk around the side of the house.

"You're not worried about him crossing the road?" Spock was a beautiful dog. It would be heartbreaking if something happened to him going between the two places like that.

Micah shrugged. "Corban isn't. He says Spock has more sense than to dart in front of a car. So far, I have no cause to question it. Honestly, the last time I watched him, it seemed like he looked both ways."

"Smart dog." They were walking past a barn now. The doors were shut tight, but no animal sounds came from inside. "What's in there?"

"Tractor storage, tools, that kind of thing. No cows, if you were worried."

She shrugged. "I'm not precisely *scared* of cows. They're just weird. You have to admit they're weird."

Micah chuckled. "Only to those of us who didn't grow up around them."

They strolled in silence for several more minutes until they came to a white picket fence. Micah pushed open the gate and gestured for Serena to go in. She looked at the riotous blooms on the bushes that made a hedge around the outside of the garden space against the fence. A bench sat at an angle by the waterfall that trickled peacefully in the corner.

"This is amazing." Serena reached out to run a finger over one of the rose petals on the bush. "Who put it here?"

He smiled and gave her hand a gentle tug. She followed him to the bench and sat. He slipped his arm over her shoulder. "Corban's mom. She apparently needed something softer, less farm-like in her life. Corban proposed to Ruth out here. Sometimes they slip over and sit on the bench like this in the evenings if no one is at the B&B. It's cute."

She turned to look up at him and had to catch her breath. He was so handsome. When her heart calmed down, she smiled. "And you know this, how?"

He gave an impish grin. "I'm a little brother. I have my ways."

Serena laughed. She didn't have siblings and had always felt she was missing out. Maybe that wasn't true after all. "Brat."

"Yeah, well. Old habits, you know?" He cleared his throat. "So...?"

Right. He wasn't visibly nervous unless you looked closely. Definitely time to talk. Where did she start? Where was the beginning? "I told you it's nothing bad."

"And yet, you keep stalling."

A chuckle escaped. "Okay. So. Um. You met my parents, the first day we met. They've been after me to come back to L.A. since, well, basically the day I left.

They don't understand—anything, honestly. They didn't know about Derrick and me. They figured he was another publicity stunt. And my faith...they stop just short of ridicule. Mom always asks when I'm going to give up on my Jesus phase and come back to the family business."

Micah winced and rubbed her shoulder. "That's got to be hard. I'm sorry."

Serena nodded. "So, anyway. Because of that, Mom, in particular, is always on the lookout for something that will tempt me to come back. Long story short, she had someone send my agent a script. I got it Friday but didn't even open it until this afternoon."

"You said before you're not interested in going back, right?"

She nodded. "I'm still not sure if I am. But, Micah, I read the script today. I...I don't know. It's a really, really good part."

After a moment, a delighted smile bloomed on his face. "You're considering it? That's great."

Great? Why would it be great? She drew her brows together. "If I took it, I'd be gone for months."

"And I'd miss you. But you're an incredible actress. Your pottery is special, too, don't get me wrong. But God gave you a talent and it seems wrong not to use it when the right opportunities come up. It's not as if doing this movie would mean you had to close your studio permanently and move back to California, right? You'd just be there for the filming and whatever. But you could come back home after." His hand continued to move up and down her arm in slow, soothing strokes.

It was the same thing Gloria had said. Why wasn't it something she'd considered? Partly because her parents had always lumped the two together—take a part and move back to L.A. Could she do it if she maintained her base here? Would that somehow keep her more centered? More able to stay true to her faith? "Just like that? You think I should do it?"

"I think you should at least consider it. Pray about it. I'll pray with you." He leaned close and pressed a kiss to her cheek. "You're right, that wasn't bad."

"There's one more little thing."

"Oh?"

"The guy at the gardens? The photographer?"

"Yeah? He was at church today, too. What about him?"

He'd been at church? How had he known which one she'd go to? She swallowed. Maybe he'd take this as well as he had the possibility of her doing a movie. "He's paparazzi."

"What do you mean? Like those people who chase celebrities? Why...what...how?"

She smiled in spite of herself. "Basically. I called my agent this morning. She thinks maybe the admin who mailed me the script slipped my address to the guy and let him know what was in the package. I'm guessing it'll show up online somewhere tomorrow. I'm sorry."

"Why?"

Did he not understand? "You're going to be in those pictures. There's going to be speculation about who you are, how long we've been together, all of that. People will probably come out to Arcadia Valley and it could get ugly. I won't blame you if you want to keep your distance."

He shook his head. "I don't want to do that. I like what we've started here. I'd like to see where it goes. Even if it's completely different than any other relationship I've had."

Serena smiled and laid her head on his shoulder. How could he accept her, and all the baggage that came with her, just like that? It was unlike anything she'd ever experienced. "Thank you."

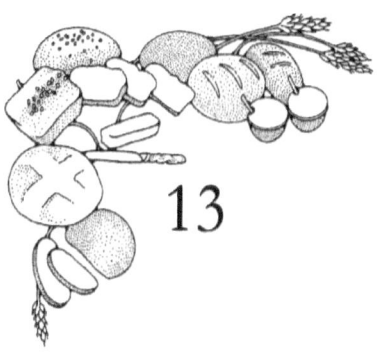

13

What had he been thinking? Micah had expected one, maybe two, photographers would come to town trying to get a story on Serena. And okay, sure, he'd been with her—had even kissed her cheek, and that photo had appeared on all the major gossip blogs on Monday—but why did people think he was a story? He was simply a baker in the process of falling in love with an amazing woman.

His hand paused on the lock to the front door. Falling in love? Was he? He was attracted to her, certainly. But it was more than that. He genuinely liked her. He liked being around her—whether they were talking or sitting in comfortable silence. He could easily picture the rest of his life with her in it.

"You going to open up or what?" Jonah crossed the bakery's front room and peered out the window. "Looks safe."

Micah snorted and flipped the lock. "For now. I'm sorry this is so crazy. I know you and the rest of the family didn't sign up for it."

"Please. Serena seems like a great girl, and you're good together. I kind of figure if you can survive this, you'll be able to survive anything. Plus, it's not like a little free publicity for the bakery is a bad thing."

"She says this is just a tiny taste. And she doesn't even have the part yet, although I guess she's been talking to the director, and it's down to formalities at this point." Micah rubbed the back of his neck as he headed toward the coffee. "Sounds like she might head out there for her parents' Fourth of July party after all."

"Bummer. We were planning on all watching the fireworks again—maybe doing another grill out. She can't go after? Or fly back in time?"

Micah shrugged. "I'll ask, but I guess she figures it's a good excuse to reconnect with some of the people she knows and meet her costars."

Jonah nodded but said nothing.

"Anyway. I think she's bringing the plates and mugs over this afternoon. I can't wait to see how it all turned out. She's been tight-lipped about the whole project."

"Make sure Malachi cuts her a check before she leaves." Jonah knocked on the kitchen door as he pushed through it back into the kitchen.

Micah scrubbed his hands over his face. He didn't want Serena to go. Here, when no one was around, he could admit that. Telling her she should and that he was proud of her wasn't a lie, though. It would just be better if there was a way for her to do that and stay here. With him.

The door swung open and a woman stepped in, followed by a man carrying a duffel bag. Micah drew in a deep breath and forced a smile. "Good morning. Welcome to A Slice of Heaven, how can I help you?"

"Oh, you're too perfect." She smiled and strode past the display cases to the cashier, her skinny heels clicking on the floor. Hand outstretched she added, "I'm Madeline Warner. You're Micah Baxter, right?"

He took her hand, trying to place the name that rang with dull familiarity in his ears. "Yes. What can I do for you?"

"You'll need to stop asking that question before much longer or people are going to take you up on it." She turned to look down the rows of bakery treats. "Are those snickerdoodles?"

"Yes, ma'am. Would you like one? Maybe some coffee?" Presumably the woman would get around to why she was there, and if he could make a sale, then so much the better. That name, though. He knew it from somewhere.

"I can't resist a snickerdoodle. Or coffee. It smells amazing in here. You do all your baking onsite?"

Micah moved to the display case and picked up a pair of tongs. "We do."

"Make it six cookies. Maybe I'll share with Max if he stops chattering so much." She flashed a grin at the silent man beside her. "Coffee?"

The man nodded.

Micah set six cookies into a small box and took them down to the cash register. He rang up the order and told her the total before gesturing to the coffee station. "You can fix your drinks over there."

Max shrugged and headed that direction, stopping to set his duffel down by one of the small tables they kept for folks who wanted to sit inside and eat.

Madeline handed him a twenty dollar bill. "Keep the change."

Micah blinked. "Ma'am?"

"You're going to earn it." She scooped up the box and headed to the table.

Micah shrugged and dropped the change into the tip jar. He and his brothers split whatever was in there between them, but it wasn't usually very much. "Thanks."

"Won't you join us?" She patted a chair.

This was getting weird. Finally, the name flashed into his brain. Madeline Warner. From Warner's Warnings, a gossip blog that became so successful she now had a TV show and several monthly columns in magazines. His heart sank. Serena hadn't been wrong. If Madeline Warner was here, the rest of the pack wasn't going to be too far behind. "No, thank you."

Madeline watched him as she stirred the coffee Max had set in front of her.

Micah offered a tight smile and sat on the stool behind the cash register. He picked up his e-reader and flicked it on. "Let me know if you need anything else."

She laughed.

Max murmured something and unzipped his duffel.

Micah read the same paragraph twice before turning his device off. "Look. I'm not sure what you're here for, but if you're looking for some kind of scoop about Serena, you can pop a lid on those coffees and take them to go."

"Oh, we're not here about her. We have plenty of those details already. Who we haven't heard of is the mysterious man she kisses while gardening." Madeline nibbled the cookie and closed her eyes, sighing. "These are the best I've had since my grandmother baked them for me as a child. What's your secret?"

"Lard." Micah smiled and reached for his phone. He caught the look of stunned horror on her face before she dropped the cookie. People shouldn't ask what was in something if they didn't want to know. Snickerdoodles required lard, though, if they were going to taste right. Well, shortening. And they used a vegetable-based one, not actual lard. But it was worth the slight exaggeration to see her face.

Max reached for another cookie. Apparently he wasn't turned off at the thought of an actual fat in his food.

The door opened and Dina Poncetta came in with her daughter, Isabella. "Hi, Micah. I'm here for my order and—oh, are those snickerdoodles?"

Micah grinned. "Sure are. Grandma's recipe."

"No wonder they're so good. Better throw in a dozen." Isabella tugged her mom's shirt and pointed to the case. Dina tilted her head and looked in. "What are those?"

"S'mores cookies. They turned out pretty well. Want to try one?" Micah slid the case open and clicked the tongs together.

"Yeah. You're going to make me add another dozen cookies to my order, aren't you?"

He chuckled and offered her a chocolate cookie filled with chunks of graham cracker and marshmallows. "Hope so. We make the marshmallows by hand."

"Homemade?" She split the cookie in half and handed part to her daughter before taking a bite. "Ohhh. This is sinful. Where do you get your ideas?"

He shrugged. This one had come from a random conversation about the big Fourth of July celebration at the park that was in the works. Ruth and Jonah were putting their heads together about treats to take for the community to share after the ball game. He started boxing up the cookies. "They're everywhere, if you look hard enough."

"Only if you're a genius in the kitchen. Whenever you and Jonah decide to settle down, you're going to have lucky wives."

Heat crawled up his neck and he fought the urge to peek over at the gossip reporter. No doubt this was making for interesting copy in her mind. He added the boxes to the reusable bag that held her weekly bread order. "Thanks."

"Here's last week's bag."

Micah took it and her credit card for the cookies. Isabella shoved the last of her cookie into her mouth and gave Micah a chocolatey grin. He handed the card and receipt back to Dina. "Have a great day."

"You, too. It was good to see you at the garden on Saturday. Will we see you out there again? There's always something to do."

"More than likely."

Dina smiled and took her daughter's hand. "See you."

Madeline brought her coffee over and leaned against the counter. "So. You give free samples to everyone?"

"Only regulars. Did you need something else?"

"No, I don't think so. Just understand, if you don't want to give us the story, I'm sure we can find someone who will. Small towns are like that." She drained the last of her drink and offered him the empty cup before gesturing to her cameraman. "C'mon, Max."

Max shrugged and grabbed the cookie box. He gave Micah a mock salute and followed after his boss.

Micah waited until the door closed and they'd crossed the parking lot before he let his smile fall away. Serena was worth it, no question, but busybodies butting into his personal life were not high on his list of things he wanted to experience. Ever. Still, he probably ought to warn her that they were in town. He picked up his phone and tapped in a text. Hopefully that wouldn't keep her from coming into town this afternoon.

He wanted to see her.

Micah glanced up as the door opened. His shoulder sagged. It was just Gloria.

"How's it going?"

"Pretty typical. Malachi's out on deliveries, Jonah's milling some flour in the back, you know. Want me to get him?"

She shook her head. "Serena said she was on her way with the plates and mugs. I wanted to see how they turned out. The way she talked about them, I'm thinking they're amazing."

His heart leapt. She was finally on her way. "I'm looking forward to seeing them myself. Do you have any details on when she's leaving?"

"No. She was going to make arrangements today, last I heard. So maybe she can fill us in." Gloria glanced out the window. "That looks like her. I'll see if she needs help."

Micah crossed to the door behind Gloria and followed her to Serena's car. "Hey, you."

Serena grinned and wrapped her arms around him. "Hi. Anymore looky-loos?"

"Nope. Just the two." Micah reached into the trunk and grabbed the larger of the two boxes inside.

"What are you two talking about?" Gloria reached for the second box.

Serena swatted her hand. "Go grab the door. Just some gossip hounds looking for a story."

Gloria's eyebrows lifted but she said nothing.

Inside the bakery, Micah set the box down on the table and reached for the lid.

"Nuh-uh. Let me." Serena grinned. "Close your eyes."

"Should I get my brothers? Well, Jonah? Mal's out still, I think." Micah glanced toward the kitchen.

"I'll go get him." Gloria pointed at Serena. "No showing until we get back."

Micah watched Gloria push through the door into the kitchen then tugged Serena close. He pressed his lips to hers, and tangled his fingers in her hair.

She sighed and leaned into him, her arms wrapping around his waist.

"Ahem." Jonah drilled a finger into Micah's shoulder. "I was told there were plates and cups to come see."

"Sorry. I didn't realize I was supposed to take longer." Gloria shook her head.

Micah's face burned.

Serena just smiled and kissed him again, lightly, before opening the box. She reached in and pulled out a newspaper-wrapped ball. "So, I couldn't get the mugs to work like I wanted with the built clay. I'll have to experiment some and see if I can figure out the right way to do it. Still, I wanted the design to match, so I painted it on instead. It's not on the inside, but that probably doesn't matter."

Micah reached for the paper as Serena unwound it to reveal a cobalt blue mug. Two loaves of golden-brown bread speared up from within the beige basket painted on the side. "I like that."

Jonah nodded. "They're great. Mal's gonna flip."

"In a good way, right?" Serena pulled out a flatter package and began to unwrap it.

"Definitely." Jonah took the mug from Micah and studied it. "These are dishwasher safe?"

"Absolutely. You needed practical. Here's the plate."

The same design filled the center of the plate, but it was obviously a part of the pottery, not something painted on top. Micah flipped it over and saw the pattern was there on both sides. "This is the Japanese thing you do? The built clay?"

Serena nodded.

"It's cool." Jonah held out his hand for the plate. "Unique."

"Thanks." Now Serena beamed. "I'm glad you like them. I started to worry they were too cheesy."

"Nothing cheesy about these at all." Jonah set the plate carefully into the box and hefted the container. "I'll take them to the kitchen and get them washed so we can put them out tomorrow."

Gloria reached for the smaller box. "I'll help. You two can return to what we interrupted. I'll go out the back."

"You don't have to..." Micah shook his head as his brother and Gloria disappeared into the kitchen. Not that he'd object to kissing Serena again, but it wasn't something they needed to be doing in front of an enormous window that faced the street. "Alrighty then."

Serena stepped close, her hands resting on his waist. "You really like them?"

"I really do." He lowered his forehead to hers. "I don't want you to go."

She frowned. "I thought you said I should? Do you think this is the wrong thing?"

He shook his head. "No. I'm just gonna miss you."

"I'll miss you, too. But I'll be back before you know it." She pressed a quick kiss to his lips. "Two weeks, tops."

"I thought you said four to six months?"

Serena chuckled and stepped back. "Sure, once we start filming. That won't be until late July at the very soonest. Talking to Zennia, my agent, they've got nearly everything in place, but there are still a few kinks to work through. So I'll fly out, do a few meetings, hang out at my parents' party, and then come home. And I was thinking..."

Her voice held just enough wheedle that Micah imagined what came next was going to be unpleasant. "What?"

"Why don't you come with me?" She grinned, bouncing a little on her toes. "I'll have plenty of free time and I can show you the sights. And that way, you won't have to start missing me just yet."

"Go with you? To L.A." Micah blinked. It wasn't impossible, but the logistics would take some handling. Mal and Jonah could manage the bakery by themselves. The baking itself, though, would be a problem. Micah had taken over the cookies completely and most of the muffin baking. Jonah spent his whole morning focused on pumping out enough bread to fill orders and the display cases. Ruth was busy with the bed and breakfast. "I'm not sure. Jonah can't really do this all by himself. Mal doesn't bake."

Her shoulders slumped. "Oh."

"I'll talk to them and see what I can do. Maybe I could come out just for the Fourth?" Would that even be worth it? He'd miss the big celebration the town was putting on at Arcadia Creek Park. He'd planned to play on the church baseball team along with Ruth and Jonah. Not that he was amazing or anything, but he could usually manage a solid base hit.

She beamed and threw herself into his arms. "Really? That would be so great. The party's the thing I'm dreading most, but with you there it'll be so much better."

"Then I'll be there." He wasn't sure how he was going to explain bailing on the game. Maybe he could talk Corban into taking his place. Missing out on that was nothing if it meant being with Serena. They'd understand. Wouldn't they? "I'll start looking at flights and get you information when I have it."

"Let me do it for you."

"No, I got it." He shook his head. He might not be rolling in the kind of money she was, but he could afford a plane ticket when it mattered. Hmm. A last-minute plane ticket. Maybe he should've thought that one through a little longer.

"Please?" She kissed him, and for a moment, he forgot what they were talking about. "You're only coming out because of me. It's a little way for me to say thank you."

Pride warred with economy. Micah pulled his lip between his teeth. "All right. Thank you."

"This is going to be great!" Her hug was practically a squeeze. "I need to run. I have a few things to mail before I head home to pack, and I'd like to try and get to bed at a reasonable time. My flight leaves at six thirty tomorrow morning."

"Can I take you to the airport?" Micah's heart ached and she hadn't even left yet.

She frowned. "I'm sorry. Gloria's taking me. I didn't even think...with the bakery and everything."

He shrugged. "You're not wrong, I'll be here. But I would've figured out a way to get out of it to see you off."

"You're sweet. I should run. Love you. I'll text you as soon as I land." Serena pressed a kiss to his lips before she spun and hurried on her way.

Micah's mouth opened but there weren't any words. The words had been so casual, careless even. Clearly she hadn't meant them. Things like that just popped out sometimes. Right?

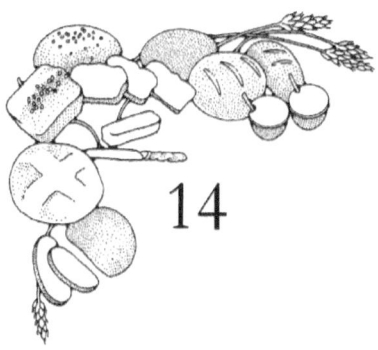

14

Serena paced by the sliding doors and looked down the crowded corridor. She'd arranged to meet Micah by the exit to this parking garage, but the airport was big and complex. It'd be easy to get turned around and end up in the wrong spot. She checked her phone. No messages or texts. The airport website said his plane had landed on time, as did the monitors at the end of the hall that she'd checked when she first arrived. So what was the holdup?

Squinting, she focused on a tall man headed her way. There he was. The tension in her shoulders and back eased and she grinned as she waved. He matched her grin and increased his pace.

"There you are." Micah pulled her into his arms and lifted her off the ground. "I've missed you. I know it's ridiculous, but that doesn't seem to matter."

"If you're ridiculous, then so am I." Serena held his face in her hands and met his lips. The crazy noise of travelers making their way to their cars and the incessant broadcast announcements faded as she lost herself in him. Here was home. Not Idaho. Not L.A. Micah. Her heart swelled until it felt like it would burst. *Thank you,*

Jesus. The prayer came out of nowhere, but it was the only concrete thought in her head. Reluctantly, she eased back. "We should go."

Micah set her on her feet and kissed her one more time before hitching his backpack higher on his shoulder. "Lead on."

Serena kept his hand firmly in hers as they threaded their way through the rows of parked cars to the space she'd managed to snag.

Micah's eyebrows lifted. "Nice."

"It's my dad's. I felt like a kid asking to borrow it, but it didn't make sense to rent a car when he has eight of them sitting around at home. Of course, the fact that I took a taxi from the airport instead of hiring a limo gave my mother heart palpitations." Serena clicked the button to unlock the doors on her father's sporty convertible. "It's a nice day. Want to put the top down?"

He nodded, a slow grin spreading over his features. "I really do."

Serena laughed and popped open the trunk. "Drop your bag in there and climb in. I'll give you the nickel tour on our way to the house. I'm glad you're able to stay tonight."

"Me, too. Even if I only have until tomorrow evening." He put his backpack into the trunk and closed it.

Serena slid behind the wheel and started the engine while Micah got situated. She pushed the button to open the convertible top and grinned. "Ready?"

"Sure. Tell me about your week while you drive."

She laughed. "There's nothing more than what I said when I called you, really."

"So tell me again. It's fun to hear you talk about it. It's a whole new side to you—and it's a glimpse into the behind-the-scenes of a movie that most of us don't get." He twisted in his seat so he was angled toward her.

Was it a different side of her? She didn't see it that way. "I'm still the same me. You're sure it's not boring?"

"Yep."

Shaking her head, Serena paid for the parking and headed out into L.A. traffic. While she drove, she alternated between pointing things out and rehashing the table reading of the script. Her costars had ranged between shocked and surprised when she'd shown up the first day. She hadn't worked with any of them before— they were all much higher on the food chain than she'd been before her five-year absence. But they'd been nice. Welcoming, even. "It's a good mix. Everyone has a solid grasp on their role. The director seems pleased. Honestly, if it keeps up this well, it'll be one of the fastest movies ever filmed."

"That'd be nice. Then you could be back home before Thanksgiving." He reached over and rubbed her leg. "When does everything start for real?"

She ran through the timeline in her head. She'd wanted to hold off on this conversation—it was sooner than she wanted. "August."

He let out a breath. "Wow. Okay. How long do you think it'll be?"

"Realistically? Maybe mid-December." She signaled and changed lanes, slowing as the road began to curve, hugging the Pacific coast. "I'm sorry."

"Don't be. This is what you want, right?"

Was it? She wouldn't go that far, necessarily, but the more she prayed about it the more it felt like this was where God wanted her. And maybe that meant it was the same thing. She nodded. "Yeah. But I was happy where I was, too."

"And you'll come back between projects and be happy there again. You have talent, Serena. Why wouldn't God want you to use it?"

She slowed, signaling a turn into a gated driveway. She had talent with clay, too, didn't she? "When I came to Arcadia Valley, I was broken. I don't think I can explain just how badly. Between my pottery and Gloria hounding me toward Jesus, and finally accepting what He had for me, I figured out that I mattered, regardless of what I did or didn't do as a career. So now, every time I sit behind that wheel, I think of God and how He's portrayed as the potter and we're clay and I'm grateful that He'd care about someone with the history I have. Back home, I don't have to watch what I do or worry about how I'm living. I can just be Serena Johnson, saved by grace. I don't want Hollywood to diminish that."

Micah nodded. "I get that. But what if, now that you have your feet solidly under you, God's asking you to step out and shine the light He put inside you, instead of keeping it to yourself?"

Serena sighed. He was probably right. She'd felt God's nudge to witness more overtly to her parents. And she'd ignored it. "I don't know if I can."

"You don't have to. Let God do it through you."

Her eyes filled and she blinked back the tears. It was hard to give up control and the security of knowing she was in charge. But wasn't that the bottom line of the Christian life when the rubber hit the road? "Yeah. Pray that I can, would you?"

"Of course."

Serena smiled and pressed the button on the garage door opener. "Home sweet home. Dad'll probably be out in less than a minute to make sure I didn't scratch his baby."

"You grew up here?"

She nodded. "Not sure I appreciated it."

He chuckled. "No one does. I might not have had tennis courts and...was that a putting green?"

"Yeah, Dad went through a phase where he was going to golf. I doubt he's been out there in the last seven years though." Serena put the top back up and turned off the engine. "Unless he crosses the grass to get to the beach stairs."

Carl Johnson poked his head out through a door and grinned. "I thought I heard my baby. How'd she do?"

Serena laughed and looked at Micah. "See? The car's fine, Dad. Thanks for letting me take it out."

He held out his hand and Serena dropped the keys into it. "You know you can always take any of the cars while you're in town. Mom has a nice new sedan over there you should try out next." He moved his gaze from the cars to Micah. "We've met?"

"Yes, sir. Micah Baxter. We met briefly at Serena's, for her kiln opening." Micah stuck out his hand.

"Of course, of course. Good to see you. Glad you could make it out for our little shindig." He shook Micah's hand. "Got your bag?"

"Oh. It's in the trunk, Dad. Pop it open?"

He pushed a button on the key fob and the trunk lid lifted. Micah reached in and grabbed his backpack before gently closing it.

"Excellent. Your mother's inside giving the caterers a heart attack. Be sure you say hello before you take him and get him settled in your room."

"What?" Serena's heart stopped. Her parents expected Micah to share her room. Of course they did. No matter how many times she explained that that wasn't how she was living her life now, they didn't believe her. Her eyes darted to Micah. What must he be thinking? "I figured I'd put him in the yellow guest room."

"Oh? Well, check with your mother. I don't think we have anyone planning on staying there, but it's always a good idea to be sure. It's a long way away from your room though." Her dad lifted a hand in a semi-wave as he turned.

"I'm sorry about that."

Micah slipped his hand into hers and squeezed. "It's fine. If the guest room doesn't work out, I can always find a hotel. There's probably something nearby, right?"

"Probably not tonight. It's the Fourth of July. There are ten bedrooms in this house, I'm sure we can find one for you to use. If not, you can take mine and I'll sleep on the couch in Dad's study." Serena tugged him toward the door that led into an enclosed breezeway connecting the garage to the main house. "Let's go say hi to Mom and see what's what."

Serena glanced over the shoulder of the studio executive who was yammering at her and smiled. Micah had been cornered at one of the drink stations by one of the younger stars on Dad's soap. That girl—what was her name?—was a menace. Even though she stayed out of the gossip circuit, Serena knew about the girl's exploits. They were usually with older, married, more successful men though. Maybe she should go save Micah. She smiled and touched the executive's arm before excusing herself.

She skirted the pool, pausing to exchange greetings with a few of her parents' regular party attendees, as she made her way to Micah.

"So I just get so lonely, you know?" The woman batted her eyelashes.

Micah shot Serena a desperate look. "There you are."

"Sorry. I was trying to get away." Serena pressed a kiss to Micah's cheek and looped her arm through his with a smile at the other actress. "So glad you could make it, dear. Be sure you get some food."

The girl showed her teeth in what was probably supposed to be a smile. "Maybe I'll go do that now. It was nice to meet you, Micah. If you change your mind about my offer, come find me."

Serena waited until the actress was out of earshot before snickering. "I can only imagine the offer she made you."

"Please don't leave me alone again." Micah shuddered. "On the bright side, I'm adding a lot of names to my prayer list."

Serena grinned. "That's just the right way to think about it. Come on, we can mingle our way over toward the lawn. The crowd always thins out over there—no food or drink—we just have to avoid the shadowy areas."

"What's the prob...oh." He huffed out a breath. "It really is a different world, isn't it?"

That was exactly the problem. How was she supposed to live in this world, even if it was only for a few months at a time, and not get dragged back into the morass? "Yeah. It is. I'm not sure..."

He stopped and cradled her face in his hands. "Yes, you can. Think about what Paul wrote to the Philippians."

Serena furrowed her brow. "Is this the 'I can do all things' speech? 'Cause our pastor did a whole series last year on scripture taken out of context and that one was top of the list."

Micah laughed and kissed her. He took her hand and they continued walking away from the majority of the party. "No. I wasn't going with that one. But we'll have to stop so I can get out my phone. I don't know it completely by heart."

Serena towed him toward an empty bench at the front part of her father's putting green. "All right, let's sit and you can lay it on me."

He grinned and slipped his phone out of his back pocket before settling on the bench. He draped an arm over her shoulders and tucked her against his side while he thumbed open the Bible app with his other hand. "Let's see...yeah, here. At the end of chapter one, 'Whatever happens, conduct yourselves in a manner worthy of the gospel of Christ. Then, whether I come and see you or only hear about you in my absence, I will know that you stand firm in the one Spirit, striving together as one for the faith of the gospel without being frightened in any way by those who oppose you.'"

"That's better than the all things bit." Serena sighed and laid her head on his shoulder. "Stand firm no matter what happens. Ties in with Ephesians six, doesn't it?"

"Full armor of God." Micah brushed his lips across her forehead. "It does. God's going to be with you, every step of the way. It may not be easy—probably won't be, honestly—but if you keep your heart set on Him and commit your ways to Him, then He'll direct your path."

Her lips curved. "You have some scripture memorized. That's one of the first verses I copied onto an index card and taped to my mirror so I'd see it every day. It's a good reminder."

"It's seen me through some things. Before I moved to Arcadia Valley, I worked for a tutoring and afterschool program. It's what I thought God wanted me to do forever—I had my eyes on opening my own franchise in another five or six years. Then we got new management and one thing led to another and it all started falling apart. I started praying—hard—that God would show me what I was supposed to do. Not a week later, Jonah's on the phone with this community-supported bakery idea. In some ways, it felt like running away, but mostly? It was a clear answer from God."

She nodded. "Too bad God isn't always that clear and direct."

Micah chuckled. "True. But I'll be praying, and you'll be praying. I imagine Gloria and the rest of my family will be, too."

Knowing Gloria, she'd have the whole church praying. Serena sighed. With that many people on her side, she had to believe God would make it clear if she took a wrong step.

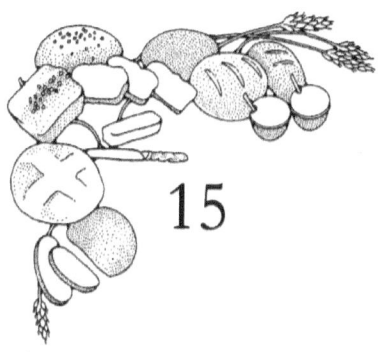

15

Micah leaned against the railing and studied the fake mammoth frozen as if struggling to get free of the black tar that surrounded it. Who knew L.A. had an active archaeological dig right in the middle of the city? Probably everyone but him. Serena had laughed when he'd asked to come, but they'd spent the morning playing tourist already—visiting the Griffith Observatory, Grauman's Chinese Theater, and strolling along the boulevard there looking at the stars—so why not one final stop? If he'd had the time, he would've asked if she wanted to go to the amusement park for the day, but that was silly when they couldn't use every hour on their tickets. They could do that another time. Maybe he could swing a weekend during filming to come see her—there had to be some way to make it work.

Serena held up their tickets and a brochure. "We're all set."

"I wish you would've let me pay."

"Nope. My treat. If we go visit D.C., you can pay then."

"The museums in D.C. are mostly free. I'm getting the better deal."

She laughed and kissed him. "Why don't we call it a tie? I get to spend the day with you, after all."

He shook his head and slipped his arm around her waist. "What's first?"

"Let's do the museum first." She pointed to the entrance. "Then see what sounds good."

A group of teenagers huddled near the entrance giggling as they passed by. One of the girls did a classic double take before whipping out her phone and snapping several photos while she jammed an elbow in her friend's side.

Micah sighed. That had happened all over town. Not a lot, but enough that he'd started noticing the way people watched and grabbed their phones. They probably thought they were being sneaky. Serena didn't even bat an eye. "Doesn't it bother you even a little?"

Serena paused in the doorway to the museum. "What?"

"The pictures?" He jerked his head toward the teens who were now all staring in their direction. Probably trying to figure out who Micah was. Or, given the situation in Arcadia Valley last week, they probably already knew. "It's just weird."

"You get used to it." She squeezed his hand. "I promise. Just ignore them. Most people are content to take a picture and leave it at that."

Like he had any other options. He forced a smile and followed her to the first exhibit. At least in here it was relatively empty. Seemed like most people were content to see the tar pits and the fake animals and leave the museum alone. He cleared his throat. "Can I ask you something?"

"Of course." Serena was leaning over a display, staring intently at a fossil. She turned her head to see him and frowned. "What's wrong?"

He was already botching it. His palms were damp and his heart was racing like he'd guzzled an entire pot of coffee. "Last week, before you flew out?"

She grinned and stepped close. "I was wondering if you were ever going to ask about that. This isn't exactly the place I would've chosen though. The observatory, now that's open and romantic. But I guess fossils will do—they last for a long time, so they've got that going for them."

Micah blinked. "I'm con—"

"Yes. I love you, Micah Baxter." Serena leaned up and pressed a kiss to his lips. "Now come on, let's go see the saber-tooth tiger. I think it's this way, but it's been a long time since I was here."

Words stuck in his throat so he followed along, letting her lead him by the hand like a puppy. She loved him. That seemed fast. They'd known each other what, six weeks? Except...hadn't he just been planning a future with her in his mind? Would he do that if he wasn't at least half in love with her? He certainly never had with anyone else.

"There he is." She grinned at Micah and stopped in front of a skeleton labeled saber-toothed cat. "Look at those teeth. They're amazing, aren't they?"

"Yeah. Though it's frustrating that all the descriptions are steeped in the idea that there are billions of years of whatever going on."

Serena angled her head. "You think there were saber-tooth tigers in Eden with Adam and Eve?"

Micah shrugged. "Of course."

"Dinosaurs?"

He stiffened. "There are plenty of fossils that show a human footprint right beside dinosaur tracks, and science says they were made at the same time. At the end of the day, I'm content to say that science can't prove conclusively one way or the other, which leaves us with faith. And when it comes to faith, I'm going to put mine in the Bible rather than the questionable pontificating of Charles Darwin."

"And that's one reason I love you. I'm not sure I've given the whole thing much thought. I grew up believing the theories I was taught in school. Maybe I need to spend some time questioning that."

Micah relaxed a little and shook his head. "Honestly? I'm not sure why. It's something people like to bring up and debate when, at the end of the day, it doesn't change the fact that God made it all. Jesus still died for our sins. He still requires us to put our faith in Him for salvation. Unless you're going to argue with a whole bunch of people who are out to prove that the Bible is just a fantasy as a means of discounting what you believe, there's really no point."

"I just might be in that position." She tugged his hand and they moved to the next set of fossils.

He hadn't considered that. There was no question her faith would be under attack while she was in Hollywood. That was simply what the culture here demanded. "I'll send you some links. You can read up in your spare time." He took a deep breath. "And for the record, I love you, too. Do you think there'll be any big steps in our relationship you'll let me take the lead on?"

"I promise to let you propose. Provided you don't take too long." She grinned and put her arms around him. "I wish you didn't have to leave today."

Micah held her tightly. "Yeah. Me, too."

"You don't have to walk me in. I know airports are a pain." Micah sighed as they exited the freeway.

"Nope. I want every last minute with you that I can have." She reached over and grabbed his hand.

"Well, I'm not going to argue. I was trying to be nice."

"Noted. Brownie points added." She glanced over at him and grinned. "Sorry we're stuck with Mom's old car."

Micah snorted. It was a nicer car than he'd ever own. "It's a fine piece of German engineering. I'm not sure why you're so down on it."

"It's just so...expected." She shrugged. "At least Dad's cars are fun."

"Being with you is fun. Don't really care about the car."

"Aww." She grinned. "That's just the right thing to say. I should be back in Arcadia Valley this weekend, middle of next week at the latest. Then they won't need me here in L.A. until the end of the month. So it's not too long. You call whenever you want. Or text."

"It's not the same. But you can count on it." He wasn't going to dwell on it, at least not for the last few minutes they had together. "Thanks for having me out. Your parents put on a pretty amazing party."

Serena laughed. "It's one of their skills, certainly. I think this is the first one I've ever enjoyed."

"I find that hard to believe. You have quite the reputation as a party girl." He grinned. Hopefully she realized he was joking.

"Yeah, yeah. Most of that was me simply trying to figure out why I felt so empty inside." Serena pulled into a parking spot and switched off the engine. "And if we're being completely honest, this is the first of my parents' parties since I was...oh, let's say fifteen...that I woke up without a hangover. It's a good change."

He grinned. "I'll have to agree with that."

She sighed heavily.

"Hey, you all right?"

"Yeah. I'm good. Just missing you already." She leaned over the center console and kissed his cheek. "Let's get you inside and checked in. We probably have time to get a little snack before you need to hit security."

Micah studied her for the space of several heartbeats before nodding. "Sounds like a plan. I love you, Serena."

Her grin melted his heart and made him wish he could stay. Or that she could head back home with him right then. "I love you, too."

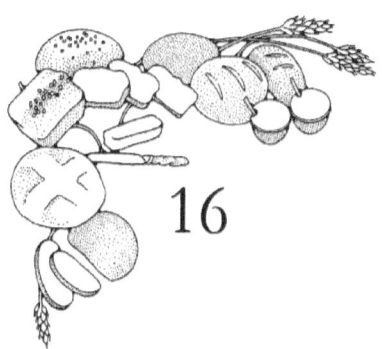

16

Serena pulled her car into a parking spot in front of the bakery. She'd only been in L.A. a few days after Micah left, but she ached to see him. She had a suitcase full of dirty laundry, more orders than she was confident she could fill in the next two weeks, and the lure of her own house waiting for her, and yet here she was.

The door chimed as she pulled it open and Micah looked over from where he stood filling a mug with coffee. His whole face brightened. He set down the drink and strode across the bakery, wrapping Serena in his arms. "You're back."

She laughed as he spun her in a small circle. "I am. For just over two weeks."

"I know, I know. Too short. Don't remind me." He pressed his lips to hers.

Serena sighed and leaned into his embrace. Home. It was the only word to describe it. She leaned back and smiled. "I missed you."

"Don't tell my brothers, because they'll say it's ridiculous, but I missed you, too. What am I going to do when you leave for four months?"

"Visit me. A lot." She wasn't going to dwell on the time apart that loomed on the horizon. She'd had too many relationships in the past that hadn't been able to weather the difficulty of conflicting filming schedules. What was it going to be like trying to juggle a normal life like Micah's with the craziness of hers? "One of the things I was waiting for was the schedule. I have a copy in my bag in the car. Maybe after I have a chance to unpack and get settled, you could come over and we can go through it and see when you can come out?"

"Absolutely. Want me to bring dinner?" He rubbed his hands up and down her arms. "Or we could go out? I can see if we can get a table at L'Aubergine finally."

Tempting. She'd gone by herself several times since she moved to Arcadia Valley. Their food was so delicious. But the thought of going out again once she got home didn't appeal. "Rain check on that. In fact, why don't you get us a reservation for just before I leave? It can be like a little going away party."

"I'm not sure I'll be celebrating that." He frowned. "But I'll see what I can do. That reminds me, though. Ruth wants to have an *actual* going away party for you. Just something small—our family, including Ursula and Corban of course, and then Pam and Emerson and Gloria, if she can swing it. She was hoping to do it your last night here, unless you have other plans?"

She'd tentatively planned to spend her last evening alone, soaking in the solitude of her house and studio, but that could also lead to brooding. Brooding was never a good thing. "Sure. That sounds great. Do you need me to come up with a few other names so Gloria doesn't feel like we're trying to force her and Jonah together?"

Micah snorted. "I'm pretty sure that's exactly what Ruth is trying to do. And honestly, I don't have a problem with it. They're good together. Even if they are both too boneheaded to realize it."

Gloria insisted she wasn't ever going to marry. Should Serena mention that? Maybe take some of the pressure off? She didn't have the answer to the inevitable question of why. Gloria kept her reasons close and had only shared little hints here and there before changing the subject. Probably better to leave it alone. "I can't say I disagree. They look good together and seem to get along, but..."

"I know, I know." Micah shrugged. "Still, they're friends. Surely friends ought to be able to get together and have fun without feeling pressured to pair up if they're set against it."

Unless they were the only unpaired people at the party. Still, it wasn't her problem to solve, if it even was a problem. "Sounds good. Have Ruth call me with the time and let me know what I can bring."

"She's not going to let you bring anything. You know that, right?"

Serena chuckled. "I have to offer. It's ingrained."

"Fair enough." The phone on the wall behind the cash register began to ring and Micah sighed. "I should grab that. I'll see you tonight?"

"Absolutely." She meant to keep the kiss brief, but found her hands slipping around the back of his neck.

With a sigh full of regret, Micah stepped back. "Go. I'll see you soon."

Right. Go. She forced her lips to curve and headed back out to her car. At least the prospect of Micah coming over tonight motivated her to work quickly. She didn't need anything hanging over her head nagging at her when he arrived. Although...maybe having a work-related distraction would keep her from thinking about how easy it'd be to let things go too far. Not that Micah was likely to let that happen, thank goodness, but he was certainly a temptation.

Whistling cheerily, Serena stepped out onto the deck with a giant mug of tea steaming in her hand. She'd slept better the previous night than she had the whole time in California. There was something to be said for being in your own bed. She took a sip and let her gaze wander over the little plot of land that had claimed her heart almost the instant she'd set eyes on it. What was she going to do for four months in L.A.?

At least she and Micah had worked out a reasonable plan for visits last night. If the movie stayed on schedule—and she'd tried to make it clear just what a big if that was—there was at least one weekend a month they could spend together. Sometimes there were even two. She could probably even make it back to Arcadia

Valley for Malachi and Ursula's wedding over Labor Day. That was the closest to a sure thing, given that it was so early in the process. Everything else was tentative, but having a plan helped ease her mind. Now, like Micah had said, they just had to put it in God's hands and trust that if He wanted them together, He'd help it work out.

Talk about stepping out in faith.

When her tea was gone, she took the mug back inside before heading over to unlock her studio. She hadn't been kidding when she'd told Micah the list of orders she had was more than she was certain she could finish before she had to leave. If she threw everything this week, she could glaze—and in some cases carve—over the weekend and into next week. Run the kiln at the end of next week and get everything packaged and to the post office right before she left. If everything went according to plan.

Serena snickered. Like that ever happened. Still, she had a tiny bit of wiggle room in there, and that even left evenings for Micah, because she wanted to spend as much time with him before she left as she could. Which meant she needed to get busy with her clay.

She'd taken the time yesterday afternoon to make sure her online store was in vacation mode, with a cheery note on the front page explaining where she was and that she hoped to be back in the studio in December. She'd also set up the auto reply for her business email. If there'd ever been a thought to hiding who she was—and there hadn't been, really, after all it was linked already in several places if people cared enough to look—that was all over now.

Serena lifted a block of clay out of its plastic bag and sliced off what she'd need for the first project of the day, then tucked the rest back into its wrapping before beginning the process of kneading the clay to ensure there weren't any bubbles that would wreck the pot when it was fired.

As the morning progressed, she repeated this process once more after turning the first lump into a serving bowl. She was in the process of making the body for a teapot when someone knocked on the studio door and stepped in.

"Can I help you?"

"Serena VanderMay?"

Serena bit back a sigh. She should've locked the door. And probably set out the private property signs at the end of her driveway. She slowed the wheel and removed her hands from the vessel. "That's me."

"I'm from the—"

"Let me go ahead and stop you. I'm not doing any interviews right now. If you get in touch with my agent, she can let you know when I'm scheduling media contacts. I'm only in Arcadia Valley through the end of the month, and I have a lot to get accomplished with my pottery business between now and then. I'm sorry you wasted your time." She stood and wiped her hands on her jeans.

"Well, but since I'm here, do you think you could—"

"No. Sorry. And you're on private property. Please leave. Have a good day." Serena took a few steps toward the door, her heart pounding. What if he didn't leave? Her phone was sitting by her pottery wheel, so she couldn't even get to it to call the cops without turning her back on him. That was poor planning.

The man didn't move. "Can I at least—"

"Hey, girl." Gloria rapped on the door frame with her knuckles. "Oh, sorry. I didn't realize you had company."

"He's just leaving." Serena had to force herself not to run to her friend and hug her. She looked so official in her uniform.

The man frowned and turned, his mouth snapping shut when his gaze landed on Gloria. He pressed his lips together and gave a curt nod before turning and stalking out to his car.

"So. What was that all about?" Gloria hooked her thumbs in her pockets and turned to watch the man get in his car and drive off.

Serena groaned. "I need to put the private property and no trespassing signs out again. I didn't even think about that this morning, but with my name back out there—and of course it's all getting tied to Arcadia Valley—the press is sniffing around. Usually they won't trespass."

"Why'd you let him in?"

Heat crept across Serena's cheeks as Gloria pinned her with her gaze. "I, um, forgot to lock the door. It won't happen again."

"Where's your phone? You should've been on it to either 911 or to me if he was refusing to go."

Serena pointed to the pottery wheel. "But you got here before there was an issue."

Gloria shook her head. "Five years and you've forgotten common sense when dealing with strangers."

That was close enough. It wasn't an issue, usually, in Arcadia Valley. People here were friendly—neighborly—and they respected your privacy. It was a small town and they didn't care who she was. "Yeah, well, it's coming back fast. What brings you around, other than to be my guardian angel?"

"I was hoping you had time for lunch."

Serena chewed on her lip. She needed to throw at least three more pieces today, but two were smallish. If Micah didn't mind moving dinner back an hour it would work. "Let me text Micah and then yes, I'd like that. I...have a relatively empty refrigerator, so I guess we need to head into town."

Gloria chuckled. "That's fine. I don't mean to make you cancel a date though."

Serena's fingers tapped on the screen of her phone. She shook her head. "Not cancelling—just pushing dinner back. We kind of planned on hanging every evening until I have to leave. Tonight we're going to be over at the farmhouse with his brothers—as much as we'd like to spend the bulk of the time alone, it didn't seem like the best idea."

"Smart. They won't mind eating later?"

"That's what I'm checking." Serena's phone buzzed with a response and she grinned. "He says they don't."

"Great. Let's get those signs posted before we go. Where do you keep them?"

Serena sighed. Where had she put them when she realized this wasn't the kind of place that needed them? "Let's look in the entry hall closet. I probably stashed them in there with my snow stuff. I'm really glad you came by—and not just because of the reporter."

"Yeah? 'Cause I started to worry when you didn't get in touch yesterday."

Serena hunched her shoulders. "Sorry. Settling back in and then Micah came over and—"

"I'm giving you a hard time. Come on."

Serena shook her head, locked the studio door, and followed her friend toward the house. She was excited about the movie, but L.A. would never be home again. Not compared to here.

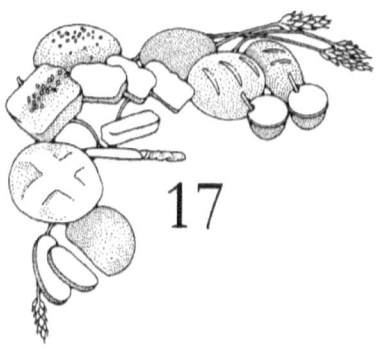

17

Micah adjusted his bowtie in the mirror before slipping his arms into the sleeves of his camel jacket. The weeks since Serena returned from L.A. had left him with a growing sense of panic. She was leaving in two days. Tonight was their last night alone. Ruth's farewell party was going to be fun and small, but it wasn't the same as a date. At least he'd finally managed to swing reservations at L'Aubergine.

"Knock, knock." Jonah leaned on the open door of Micah's room and let out a low whistle. "Looking snazzy. You sure you're not planning on proposing?"

He'd thought about it. A lot. But the reality was they'd only known each other two months. He loved her. There was no question. There was also no question that he believed fervently that Serena was the woman God had for him, but the timing was off. He didn't want her to think he was trying to put his stamp of ownership on her—like he was worried she wouldn't come back to him. He wasn't. He believed in her—in her love for him—absolutely. "It's not right yet. Maybe when the movie's wrapped."

"Listen to you, 'when the movie's wrapped.' One visit to California and suddenly you're Mr. Hollywood." Jonah's eyes sparkled with mirth. "I still think you ought to ask her. The two of you, man, you're a set. A perfect matched set. Just like Mal and Ursula and Corban and Ruth."

Micah frowned. "Hey. You'll find someone."

Jonah jerked a shoulder. "I'm not worried about that."

"Sure. I still think you and Gloria—"

"Stop, okay? Have a great time tonight."

"Yeah. Thanks." Micah watched his brother amble down the hall. He couldn't fix that, but he could do a better job praying about it. Jonah deserved an amazing woman in his life—someone who got him—someone like Gloria.

He double-checked that he had his wallet and keys and headed downstairs. Malachi glanced up from the video game he was playing and gave him a thumbs up. Micah smiled and returned the gesture. Even though he wasn't asking her to marry him, the night felt important, like it was some kind of milestone. Hopefully he wouldn't mess it up.

The drive to Serena's house was long enough to lull the butterflies in his stomach to sleep, but they all took off again when she answered the door. The simple navy blue dress hugged her curves in all the right places. Her fiery hair hung in loose waves around her face. "Wow."

A slow grin spread across her features. "You always know just the right thing to say."

Micah's mouth was dry. Looking at her, the reality of who she was landed on his chest and squeezed the breath out of his lungs.

"Hey. You okay?" She reached out to take his hand and squeezed his fingers.

"Yeah. More than. I love you, you know that?"

She leaned up and pressed her lips to his. "Backatcha."

He chuckled, his muscles relaxing. "Shall we?"

The ride to L'Aubergine went quickly. They chatted about the pots she'd made over the last two weeks, and the horror on the faces of the postal employees when she showed up with all the boxes that afternoon.

The hostess seated them in the back room against the windows overlooking what had once been the backyard when the restaurant had been a private home but was now patio seating. The space also boasted an outdoor kitchen. The whole thing could be rented for parties.

"Mal and Ursula looked at having their reception out there." Micah reached past the candle flickering in the center of the table for her hand.

"Yeah? What changed their mind?"

"Honestly? I'm not sure. I think Mal was all for it, but Ursula wanted something more like what Ruth did. And I think maybe she's worried about the weather. At the farmhouse, they can put up a tent if they need to and it's more casual, friendly." Micah shrugged. "I haven't honestly paid a lot of attention when Ursula gets going because I'll be there no matter what, so it doesn't really matter. You know?"

"You're such a guy. Tell me you'll care when it's our wedding." He smiled as red flooded her face. "I—not that—I mean—"

"I promise." He brought her hand to his lips and brushed a kiss across her fingers. "I want that, too, eventually."

Serena nodded and sipped her water. "Tell me about tomorrow night. What's Ruth got planned?"

Micah shook his head. Was she disappointed? Had she been expecting him to propose tonight? Maybe he'd missed a cue somewhere along the way, but it wasn't right yet. If Serena was going to do movies, even occasionally, he needed to know what that was like inside their relationship.

"Why aren't you picking her up again?" Ruth bustled past Micah in the kitchen at the farmhouse, pausing to scowl at him. "It just doesn't seem right."

"She wanted to drive herself. I didn't want to argue with her. If you care that much, why don't you call her and talk her into it?" Micah plucked a stuffed mushroom off the tray Ruth had just finished arranging and slid the others over to hide the missing space.

Ruth turned, frowning. "If I had more time, I would. And no more snacking. You'll get some when everyone gets here and not until then. Shoo. Go help Corban with the table or something. You're in my way."

Micah grabbed his sister and scrubbed his knuckles across the top of her head. "Thanks for doing this for Serena. I appreciate it. So does she."

"Get out of here, moron." There was laughter in her voice and the frown lines around her eyes had disappeared.

Considering his work in the kitchen done, he tossed his sister a mock salute and headed for the dining room. Corban was sitting in one of the chairs, his feet propped on another, scrolling on his phone.

"Working hard, I see." Micah pulled out another chair and sat.

"Table's set. Ruth's in a mood, so I didn't want to risk going into the kitchen to ask what else she wanted me to do. Figure she'll let me know if she needs me."

"Could've given the rest of us a heads-up about the mood. What's going on?"

Corban shrugged.

Micah pursed his lips. Shouldn't husbands know these things? Then again, he'd known his sister for twenty-nine years and still didn't have a full handle on her all the time. "Women."

Corban snickered. "Pretty much. The food smells good though, so that's a plus."

"Ruth's food always smells good. And Jonah did a lot of helping out this afternoon. I sometimes think he misses being part of a restaurant kitchen. He says he doesn't, but there's just that vibe."

"You don't think he'll want to leave, go somewhere he can get back to that, do you?" Corban leaned forward, his feet dropping off the other chair. "That would kill your sister."

Micah shook his head. He couldn't see that happening. "Nah. He's as tied to family as the rest of us are. But I could see him looking at restaurant jobs nearby. Not sure what that'd mean for me and Mal. I don't think I could do all the baking on my own...and I'm borrowing trouble."

"Never a good plan." Corban stood. "Let's go hang on the porch. People should be arriving soon."

Micah nodded and followed his brother-in-law through the house and out the front door. "It's a nice night. Maybe we can talk Ruth into dessert outside."

"I tried to convince her we should do the whole thing out here, but she was worried about bugs." Corban leaned against one of the porch posts. "I figured it was better to let her do things her way."

"And that is why you're a happily married man." Micah laughed. "At least according to what my dad told the three of us boys growing up."

"Corban! I need your help." Ruth's voice carried through the open door and Corban rolled his eyes as he headed back inside.

Micah sighed. His dad had been full of little nuggets of advice on marriage, though they mostly boiled down to keeping God as the most important thing in their lives and being willing to sacrifice their own wants for those of their wives. Sacrificial love like Jesus had for the church. Like letting Serena go make a movie— encouraging her to do it—when it was the last thing he wanted.

Would they make it? He prayed so.

Serena's car turned into the driveway. She parked and waved. Micah grinned and headed over to greet her.

"Am I late?" Serena stepped out of the car and pressed her lips to his. "I was packing, but I set an alarm."

"You're not late. You're the first person here."

Serena laughed. "Then I guess we're all right on time. Is Gloria coming?"

"Last I heard, yeah." He wound his fingers through hers. "Come on, maybe you being here will get Ruth to chill. She's been going crazy all afternoon."

"I know that feeling."

"What's going on?"

She sighed. "I'm just worried. What if I can't do it?"

He drew his eyebrows together. What if she couldn't do what? "Act? You're a great actress. My favorite, actually."

She smiled. "Thanks. But no, not the acting. I mean, I guess I'm a little worried about that, but it all came back so well during the table reads, I think that part will be fine. I mean living like I'm supposed to when I'm around so many people who don't believe in Jesus all day every day. I want to make sure I'm not the reason they turn away that final time...but I still sin. You've heard the occasional word slip out that shouldn't, and I get a little thrill still when I hear a juicy piece of gossip. None of those things are what I should be doing."

Micah wrapped his arms around her. "Nobody's perfect. And Jesus doesn't have a checklist that He's watching, making sure His followers never step out of line. Not that that gives us license to do whatever we want whenever we want. Being a Christian is all about transformation. It's about repenting when we sin and asking the Lord to help us not keep doing those things that trip us up. Do you swear on purpose?"

She shook her head.

"What about gossip? Do you seek it out and think about how much better you are than the other person involved?"

"No."

He kissed her nose. "You sin. So do I. So does everyone. The difference between a Christian and a non-Christian is that we recognize it, call it what it is, ask forgiveness, and then do what we can with God's help to get better. Sometimes I think seeing a Christian handle the sin in their life with humility and repentance is a bigger witness than someone who acts like they have it all together and tries to hide their wrongdoing."

"Okay." Serena blew out a breath. "So you're saying just be me and do a lot of praying."

He chuckled. "Basically, yeah, which, if you're like me, is how you get through every day anyway."

Another car turned into the driveway, pulling up to park next to Serena's. Pam and Emerson stepped out and gave them cheery waves.

"Hey." Emerson pulled open the back door and reached inside, emerging with a covered dish.

"Hey guys, glad you could make it." Micah squeezed Serena's hand before reaching for the screen door and pulling it open. "Come on in."

"Ruth told me there was nothing I could bring." Serena frowned at the dish as Emerson passed her and strode into the house.

Pam laughed. "She told me the same thing. I couldn't help myself. If she ends up not serving it, the boys'll be glad to have it tomorrow. It's a cherry cobbler."

"Mmm." Micah followed behind the women. "There's always a little extra space for cobbler. Don't let Ruth tell you otherwise."

They were just gathering around the table when someone banged on the screen door and a voice called out, "It's Gloria. I'm not late!"

Jonah chuckled and excused himself. A moment later they returned. Gloria still wore her uniform, but she'd loosened her hair and let it out of the tight bun at the base of her neck that she usually kept it in.

"Sorry. Maybe I'm a teeny bit late." Gloria went to stand behind the chair Jonah gestured to.

"You're right on time." Ruth smiled and nodded to Corban.

Corban cleared his throat. "Let's pray."

Micah reached for Serena's hand and listened as his brother-in-law thanked God for the food, all their blessings, and then offered a special benediction for Serena as she left them. When she sniffled, he squeezed her fingers, grateful his own eyes were closed since there was a suspicious amount of extra moisture in them. When Corban reached the end, everyone murmured "Amen" before pulling out a chair.

Food and conversation flowed easily around the table, requests for a particular dish intermingling with someone's humorous story from the past week. Micah's parents had been big fans of family suppers—where family was a loose definition that always included more people than had an actual blood relation to the Baxters. This little dinner party captured that same atmosphere perfectly—for perhaps the first time since they'd arrived in Idaho.

After everyone had eaten their fill, Ruth collected the dinner plates and she and Corban disappeared into the kitchen. They returned with a stack of smaller plates, Pam's crumble, and an enormous glass bowl filled with trifle.

"Before we get to dessert," Ruth set the desserts down on the table and reached for Corban's hand, "Corban and I have some news."

Pam grinned.

Micah glanced at his brothers. At least they looked as confused as he felt. "Is something wrong?"

"No, nothing's wrong. I—we—wanted to do this when everyone we consider family in Arcadia Valley could be here."

There was a little hitch in Micah's breath. Ruth wasn't always upfront when there was something bad going on. She'd try to spin it and make it no big deal.

Ruth blew out a breath and smiled up at her husband. His sister had found herself the perfect husband. Micah's parents would've loved Corban. "Here goes—I'm pregnant."

"What? That's awesome. Congratulations!" Micah grinned and jumped from his chair to embrace her. Malachi and Jonah had the same idea, resulting in her staggering back a few steps.

"You're going to be such a great mom. And I get to be the fun uncle. I'm calling dibs right now." Micah returned to his seat, his cheeks starting to hurt from the wide grin splitting his face.

"Fat chance. This kid's going to have three fun uncles. Right, Mal?" Jonah's excitement was evident in his voice. "Nice job, sis. You, too, Corban."

"Anyway, we wanted to tell everyone before it got obvious. I've been worrying that it wouldn't happen—I mean, we weren't not trying to get pregnant, you know?"

"Too much information." Micah grimaced. His sister was married. He got that that included sex, but it wasn't something he was going to ponder. "For all I know, Corban's going to be out harvesting cabbages in nine months and come home with a baby."

Corban laughed. "No cabbages are being harvested in April, but I get your point."

"Anyway. We're not exactly spring chickens, so I was starting to worry." Ruth cleared her throat. "Now I don't have to."

Ruth was only thirty-four. Was that old? It didn't seem old. On the other hand, Ruth had always wanted kids, so maybe it was just past the timeframe she'd envisioned. Micah's eyes burned and he blinked.

"I'm so happy for you." Pam beamed across the table at them. "Maybe if I can snuggle your new little one, I'll get over the yearning for one more that keeps stirring in my heart."

"You, too?" Emerson looked at Pam. "I thought you said we were done?"

Pam chuckled. "Oh. Well. Maybe we aren't then. I never thought you'd agree."

Emerson kissed Pam. "This kid's gonna need a playmate, you know."

Malachi and Ursula exchanged smiles.

"I suspect there are going to be plenty of playmates around." Jonah nudged Malachi in the ribs. "Once these two get married. Cousins have to be easier than siblings though."

Micah laughed. "Right. Like you'd trade any of us. If it wasn't for you wanting us all to be close, we'd probably still be in D.C."

Dessert was served with a lot of laughter, baby jokes, and sidelong glances between the couples at the table. Gloria, Ursula, and Pam followed Ruth into the kitchen after insisting they be allowed to help with the dishes. Jonah, Malachi, Corban, and Emerson wandered into the living room.

Micah turned to Serena. "It's a nice evening. Want to go for a walk?"

She shrugged. "Sure."

Her response was a little less enthusiastic than he'd hoped for, but it wasn't a no. He took her hand as they got to the front door. "It's hard to picture my sister having a baby. I mean, she's great with kids, but she's Ruth, you know?"

Serena smiled. "Yep. It's good news. Nice that they thought to include me."

Her voice was flat. Micah frowned. "Why wouldn't they? They know how I feel about you—about the future I hope we'll have together."

"Of course. I'm sorry." She stopped on the porch and wrapped her arms around his waist. She rested her head on his shoulder. "You know what? I should go. My flight's pretty early tomorrow, and I still have a little more packing to do."

"Are you sure I can't take you to the airport?" Micah's arms tightened around her. He wasn't ready for her to leave—not tonight, and not tomorrow, either.

"I'm sure. They need you at the bakery." She tipped her face up and pressed her lips to his. She pulled away as he tried to prolong the kiss. "I'll call you as soon as I land. Be sure and let Ruth know how much I enjoyed tonight, would you? I love you."

"I will. I love you, too." He walked with her down the porch steps and held the door to her car as she got in. This wasn't how he'd pictured their last evening together at all. Somewhere between her arrival and now something had happened. "Are you sure you're okay?"

"Yeah. Of course. Just a lot to do." Her smile was tight as she pulled the car door closed. She turned on the engine and rolled down the window. "Goodbye, Micah."

She put the car in reverse and Micah stepped back, lifting his hand in a wave. "'Night. Have a safe trip."

All Serena gave him was a short nod before she turned out of the driveway. The air stuck in his chest. Something about the way she'd said goodbye...he swallowed and tried to shake it off. It was like she'd said. She had a lot on her mind. Stuff to do, plus her concern about filming starting up. It was nothing. She was fine. *They* were fine.

Maybe if he said it enough he'd believe it.

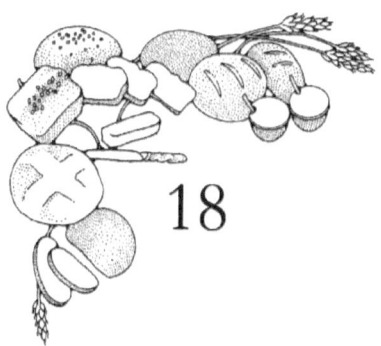

18

Serena glanced at her phone as it began to buzz. Micah again. He'd been calling and texting just like he'd said he would. And she'd done what she could to avoid him or keep their conversations short. It hadn't been hard. The first month of shooting had been intense with early morning wake up calls and late-night re-shoots. Throw in hours between her scenes memorizing lines and she hadn't exactly been sitting around with nothing to do.

Now here it was, the start of Labor Day weekend. Serena was supposed to go home tonight. Technically, she should have left last night. Ursula and Malachi were getting married tomorrow, and everyone expected her to come home.

Home.

She missed her studio.

And Micah.

She swallowed the lump in her throat and stared out at the ocean as her phone chimed with a voicemail.

Brushing away the tear that slipped down her cheek, Serena keyed in her passcode and listened.

"Hi, beautiful. I was hoping I'd catch you at lunch, but I guess they've got you working. I'm bummed that they kept you an extra day, but I'm looking forward to seeing you tomorrow—I have a little free time before the wedding. Say the word and I'll come get you at the airport. I love you. Call me when you can."

Her finger hovered over the key that would delete the message for a second before she hit save instead, as she had with all his other messages. It'd be one more thing to listen to at night when she wasn't sleeping.

"I thought I'd find you down here." Her mother slipped off her shoes at the bottom of the stairs to the beach and crossed the sand to where Serena sat. "You didn't bring down a chair? Scoot over so I can have some of that towel."

Serena moved over and looked at her mother. She'd aged well—although that hadn't been a completely natural process. Still, she wasn't one who clung to the illusion of youth at all costs. And she and Dad seemed happy enough, especially for a Hollywood marriage. "What's up? You hate the beach."

"I do. But I know you come down here when you're sulking, and I wanted to talk to you."

"I'm not sulking."

"Oh, please. That's exactly what you're doing. I'm not sure why, not when everything in your world is on the upswing—what with the movie and that nice young man. Yet here you sit when you should be at the airport doing whatever it takes to get on an earlier flight so you have more time to spend with him before heading back here on Monday."

"Are you asking me to leave?"

"No, honey, I'm asking you to live. I don't know what happened. All I know is that you left in July looking like a woman in love and you came back in August with practically the same expression you had when you realized Derrick hadn't made it."

"I haven't been that bad."

"You're not the one looking at you." Serena's mother patted her leg. "I gave you your space hoping it would help, but I can't let it go on. Not when you're sitting out here on the beach instead of getting on a plane like you planned. Whatever happened, you need to face it. Deal with it. Hiding from things just makes them worse. Your flight leaves in four hours. I've got a car coming to get you in about ninety minutes. I'll pack for you if that's what it takes, but I suspect you'd rather take care of that yourself."

"Mom." Serena's stomach dropped into her toes. "Why would you do this?"

"Because I know I haven't always been the mother you needed, or deserved. These last five years though, I've seen the woman you can be. Maybe it's maturity, maybe it's your Jesus thing. But whatever it is, I don't want to see you lose yourself again. Nor do I want you to lose Micah—I like him. He's good for you. Steady. Solid. And desperately in love."

Serena's eyes filled. "I love him, too, but I can't be what he needs. It isn't fair to let him think I can."

"I think maybe that's for him to decide. Or for the two of you to decide together." Her mother tilted her head. "Do you want to tell me what happened?"

Serena shook her head. "I just realized that he expects things from a relationship that I can't give him."

Her mother's eyebrows winged up. "I thought he was just as religious as you were and into that whole 'saving yourself for marriage' thing."

She closed her eyes. "Not those kind of things, Mom. His sister's pregnant and he's over the moon. When he looked at me, I could see it on his face. He's picturing our life together, with kids running around our feet. You know I can't...he deserves someone who can give him the things he wants—what he deserves."

"And is that what you think your God is saying, too?"

Serena stared out across the waves, not seeing anything. Her prayer life had been choked off ever since she got back to L.A. It was as if her words bounced off the ceiling and plopped into a soggy pile at her feet. "He's not saying much of anything right now."

Her mother stood and brushed sand off the back of her pants. "Well, I don't know a whole lot about religion, but maybe you should stop and think about why you can't hear Him. Don't be late. The next flight after yours is a red eye."

Why did God feel so distant? She'd read a book when she was a new believer that assured her that God never moved away from His children. So if He hadn't moved...had she?

Someone banged on the door to the pottery studio. Serena slowed the wheel and took her hands off the clay before she looked. Gloria. With a sigh, she stood and crossed to the door to unlock it. "Hey."

"Hey yourself. What's up with you?" Gloria barreled in and paced across the studio. "You take a cab home from the airport last night and now, when you could be hanging out with Micah before the wedding you're sitting here mucking around with clay."

"I happen to like 'mucking around with clay' as you so tactfully put it. And I make the bulk of my living from it." Or she used to. She could live off what she was making for the movie for quite some time. And it wasn't as if she was a pauper to start out. So maybe the money wasn't something to bring up.

Gloria shook her head. "Right. 'Cause you *need* to earn a living."

"You know what I meant. Anyway, Micah's got to be going crazy with preparations for his twin's big day. He doesn't need me in the way." Serena went back to the wheel and started it up again, squashing the little voice in her head that called her a liar.

Gloria crossed her arms. "He needs you there. The guy's been missing you like crazy. He's more excited about seeing you this weekend than his brother getting married."

"You're his spokesperson now?" She winced as the words left her mouth. She shouldn't take it out on her friend. "Sorry."

"I return to my previous question, what's up with you?" Gloria perched on one of the work tables and pinned Serena with her gaze.

"It's nothing."

"Uh huh. You forget I've known you for five years. It's going to be easier all around if you just tell me." Gloria sighed. "Or if not me, somebody. Before it eats you up inside."

It wasn't eating her up. She was working through it. Mostly. "It's complicated. And I guess I need to talk to Micah about it. I'm...just not sure I know where to start."

"You should figure it out. Sooner than later. He's worried about you. Even more now that he thinks you're avoiding him."

"Then why isn't he here banging down my door?"

Gloria smirked. "Your door is still intact. And mostly because I talked him out of it—he does have stuff to do for the wedding. Maybe that was a mistake."

Serena finished the body of the teapot she was making and stopped the pottery wheel. "No. No, it wasn't. I don't know what to do."

"Talk to me."

Serena sighed. Maybe Gloria would have something useful to add. Her mother's advice still circled in her head, but she wasn't sure how to take it. Could you get good advice from a non-believer? "Let me wash up. Go on in the house and put the kettle on. I'll be there in a few."

Gloria nodded before she left.

Serena focused on the cleanup and set the teapot body on a shelf wrapped in plastic. Why was she making something when she wouldn't be around to fire it for a long time? She ought to just smash the thing and stick the clay back in storage. Maybe tomorrow.

Gloria had a steaming mug of tea and was curled on the couch flipping through the script Serena had left on the coffee table. She looked up when Serena walked in. "This is good. I see why you wanted to do it."

"Right? And the rest of the cast is amazing. I'm not thrilled about being away from the studio for so long, but hopefully business will pick up again once I'm back."

"You know it will. Especially now that everyone knows you're not dead." Gloria grinned. "Who'd pass up the chance at an original piece of art by Serena VanderMay? You'll probably have to raise your prices to weed out the riffraff."

Serena snorted and filled a mug with water from the kettle. She chose a bag of Darjeeling and dunked it in the water. "There's a thought."

"Is it the time away that's worrying you? From what you said, the two of you worked out a pretty doable schedule for visits. I think you'll be able to make it work."

"It's not the time, although that isn't working in my favor, either." Serena sighed and settled in the chair facing the couch. Toying with the string on her tea bag, she related the talk with her mom. "It isn't fair to him. I can't let him go on thinking that there's a future with me and a big, happy family if he just waits long enough."

"So, you're just making that decision for him?"

"You saw his face, Gloria. It's the same decision he'll make as soon as I work up the courage to tell him."

"I don't think you're giving him enough credit." Gloria sipped her tea.

Maybe not, but she'd been let down for so much less so many times in the past. Not by Micah, that was true, but still. "I dunno. Can we talk about something else? How's crime here in our little slice of the world?"

Serena smoothed a hand over her skirt as she got out of her car. The parking lot at Grace Fellowship was already filling. Had they invited the whole church to their ceremony? Malachi and Ursula were both pretty involved, so it made sense. Serena just hadn't expected so many of them to take them up on the invite. She reached for the bowl she'd made them in July when she was finishing up her last batch of orders. Hopefully they'd like it. It wasn't something off their registry that they could exchange...should she have gone that route?

"Serena!"

Heat spiked through her at Micah's call and her heart leapt into her throat. Smiling, she increased her pace to meet him. The urge to be in his arms was overwhelming. "Micah."

He wrapped his arms around her. "I've missed you so much. I'm glad you could get away after all."

"Me too." She leaned back and studied his face. All of the questions and her decision to break things off faded as she looked at him. This man. How was she going to live without him? Was it really possible that he could still love her—still want her—when she told him the truth?

"I don't have a lot of time, we're almost ready to start seating people. But after? At the reception? You're all mine. Promise?" He lowered his lips to hers.

Serena closed her eyes and leaned in. Maybe it wasn't too good to be true after all. "I promise."

He smiled and released her, reaching for her hand instead. "Come on, I'll put you on the family row."

The family row. Her heart stuttered in her chest. It's what she wanted, but also what she feared. Would he—could he—still love her? She nodded. "Sounds perfect. Thanks."

The decorations were simple but lovely. Pink and white roses in small bouquets lined the main aisle, larger arrangements of the same adorned the front where the bridal party would stand and Malachi and Ursula would exchange their vows.

"It's pretty, isn't it?" Gloria, wearing a simple, pale blue linen suit, slid into a seat next to her. "Micah said it was okay for me to sit up here and keep you company, though I think you probably know a lot of the people here, too."

There were familiar faces, certainly, but the number of people she'd say she really knew...that was much smaller. "You look amazing."

Gloria shrugged. "I can clean up okay when the need arises."

Serena snorted. "Understatement of the year. I suspect a certain groom's brother will be unable to keep his eyes off you."

"I'm going to use my amazing powers of deduction to see that verbal sally as an attempt to keep me from asking if you talked to Micah. And yet, I'm undeterred. Did you?"

"Not yet. After the wedding."

"Reception?"

Serena shook her head. This wasn't a conversation to have when other people were around, or when they were supposed to be celebrating someone else's joy. "After."

"Promise me."

She sighed. It was a day for promises, apparently. "Yeah, okay."

The music started. The gentle strains of Jesu, Joy of Man's Desiring played on an acoustic guitar. The pastor, Malachi, Jonah, and Micah filed in from the side. When they were in place, Corban escorted Ursula's mother to the row across from them, then he and Ruth came to sit in the same row as Serena and Gloria. The song ended and, after a moment of quiet, the guitar started to play a simplified rendition of Bach's Sheep May Safely Graze.

Ursula's mother stood and the attendees followed suit, turning to watch as Ursula and her dad came down the aisle. Serena discreetly flipped her program over. Why hadn't Ursula chosen some bridesmaids? Even if she didn't have sisters, she surely had friends who would have stood up for her. Not that it mattered. Simple was lovely, and it reflected what she knew of both the bride and groom.

The pastor gestured for everyone to sit and the ceremony began. Serena found her gaze shifting toward Micah. He was handsome in the black suit and pale pink tie Ursula had chosen for all the men. Of course, he was handsome in jeans and a T-shirt. It wasn't just his looks—though they were nothing to discount—every piece of him drew her. Micah turned and their gazes met. Love swamped her. Why had she ever thought she could just walk away?

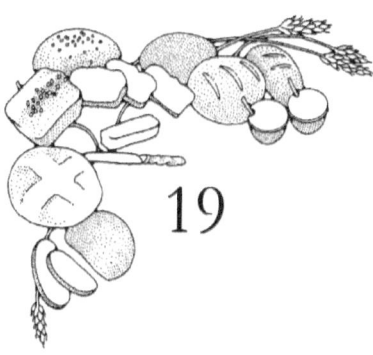

19

Micah leaned over and signed to his brother below the table so no one could see. "You're sure it's okay if I do this?"

Malachi grinned and nodded.

"Ursula doesn't mind?"

Malachi nudged his new bride with his elbow and jerked his head toward Micah.

"You're going to do it now? Awesome." Ursula beamed.

That was a pretty clear endorsement. He took a deep breath and patted the pocket of his suit jacket. The small bulge of the ring box was there, as it had been all afternoon. A tiny part of him still wondered if it was too soon. The original plan had been to wait until the movie was finished. But why wait when his decision wasn't going to change? Serena was the woman for him—he'd been praying for clarity since the trip to L.A. and the peace he had about that couldn't be denied. Micah swallowed. He could do this. He stood and gently tapped his spoon against his water goblet. "Could I get everyone's attention?"

Gradually the conversation around the open-sided tent they'd erected near the barn quieted and everyone turned his way. Micah cleared his throat. "First off, I wanted to propose a toast to my twin brother and his new bride. Ursula, you're the best thing that's ever happened to my brother—well, other than being my twin of course." He paused while people chuckled. "I'm looking forward to having you for a sister in the years ahead. And Malachi—I probably should take back all the teasing and grief I gave you about falling half in love with some person you played an online video game with. But I'm not going to because the two of you still play online together even when you're sitting in the same room. Here's to the bride and groom and their future together."

Everyone applauded and drank.

Micah cleared his throat again. "Speaking of the future...weddings are a beautiful celebration of the love between a man and a woman and the covenant they make with God and each other, and I can't think of a better time to start down that road than on the day when my brother reaches its culmination."

Micah turned to Serena. Her eyes were wide, lips parted. He got down on one knee and reached into his pocket for the box. "Serena Johnson, would you do me the very great honor of agreeing to be my wife?"

"I..." Her gaze flicked around the room and her lips curved up. "Yes. Of course."

While Micah slid the ring on her finger, people applauded. He leaned forward and brought his lips to hers. "I love you."

Serena nodded, her cheeks turning a deep pink.

Why wasn't she saying anything? Keeping hold of her hand, Micah resumed his seat and the M.C. announced that it was time for the new couple to cut their cake. Gloria, sitting on the other side of Serena, was leaning toward her, whispering intently, but Micah couldn't catch the words. Maybe asking her in public had been a bad idea. Would she have preferred for him to do it when they were alone? That had been Ruth's vote. But Micah had counted on her enjoying a little bit of the spotlight—he'd wanted to give her that and let her know he wasn't worried about what anyone else thought. She'd said yes.

Why wouldn't she meet his eyes?

Micah slowed as he approached the turn in to Serena's house and muttered under his breath. A handful of cars had pulled off on either side of the road and people inside them had cameras with long, fat lenses poking out of the windows. Why was it so much worse here than in L.A.? He turned in and parked, drumming his fingers on the steering wheel. Serena insisted that ignoring the photographers was the best course of action, but everything in him wanted to stomp out there and make it clear how unwelcome they were. They had no business here. Didn't Serena deserve to be left alone?

Grinding his teeth together, he pushed open his door and sent a fulminating look in the direction of the cameras. This late at night, it was unlikely they could see anything, so there was no point picking a fight. No matter how satisfying it might be. Why were they here, staked out, when she was only on a break from filming for the weekend? Didn't they have enough celebrities to stalk at home?

He grabbed the package he'd put together with reception leftovers off the passenger seat and strode toward the house, opting for the entrance off the deck rather than the front door. Serena was curled on the couch in the living room, staring at her hand. She jolted when he tapped on the glass.

"Come in."

He pushed the door open and smiled. She'd lit candles all around the room. They gave everything a quiet, golden glow. "Sorry it took so long. Every time I thought we had it all cleaned up, we found another problem that needed to be dealt with."

"It's okay. It's not that late."

Micah settled next to her and slipped an arm around her shoulders. "I brought you something."

"*Another* surprise?" She sounded wary.

Micah nodded and gestured for her to open the box. "It's a better surprise than the reporters parked outside on the road. Do you want me to get them to leave? Or I can call Gloria?"

She shook her head and picked at the lid of the box. "There's no point, that'll just entice them to go hiking to see if they can find a better angle. At least with them out front I know where they are."

Micah drew her closer, but she sat stiff and unresponsive. He swallowed as his stomach churned. "It's good to have you back home..."

"Micah, don't." Serena leaned away and crossed her arms. "Why did you do this?"

"Do what, exactly?" Micah clasped his hands in his lap so she wouldn't see them tremble.

"This." She held up her hand, where his diamond sparkled.

"I almost didn't. You've been...distant. It stung. I hoped you'd just been busy, and that now that you're back you'd remember what we have. What I think God put into our lives. And it was that sense of right, the peace I get whenever I pray for you—and for us—that convinced me that proposing was the right thing to do."

"You deserve so much more than me. A normal life. Isn't that what you said you wanted? What you found here in Arcadia Valley? Nothing about my life is normal, not anymore. I'm heading back to L.A. on Monday. And I don't know if I should come back. You see what it's like out there now, when filming has barely started. What's it going to be like when the movie's out? Or if I do another one down the road? You don't want to be tied to someone who's always going to be in the public eye and hounded by photographers and reporters looking for a story. To have articles written that we're on the verge of divorce because of the way I did or didn't look at you during some event? That's not your life. It's not fair for me to ask you to take it on."

Micah clenched his teeth together, biting back the retort on his tongue. "And you get to decide all of that for me?"

"If you're honest with yourself, you know that kind of life isn't what you want. It's not what anyone would call normal." Serena fumbled the ring off her finger and held it out.

Maybe it's what he'd always said he wanted, but he hadn't known any different. Normal was what *everyone* wanted until they met someone who offered them something else. Something better. "Not anymore. Not if it means I don't have you."

She closed her eyes, her head shaking. "You can't know that. This is just such a tiny glimpse of what it could be like, and you already hate it."

"Maybe that's true. Maybe it's a little annoying. But what you're leaving out is that I love you."

"For now. What happens when it gets to be too much?"

"Then we—you and I together—figure out a way to make it not be too much. Maybe...maybe we move to L.A. where the craziness isn't so obvious. Or something. Why don't we wait and solve the problem after it happens instead of anticipating what might not ever come to pass?" Blood pounded in his ears, but he focused on his breathing. Yelling at her wasn't going to help any, even if it might make him feel better. For about two seconds. Then, of course, he'd feel worse. Calm and rational. Those were the keywords to choose. Regardless of the churning in his stomach and the sense that he was teetering on the edge of an abyss with no idea if she was going to throw him a lifeline or push him over.

"I can't give you what you want, okay?" Tears spilled from her eyes and ran down her cheeks.

His heart cracked and he scooted closer, fighting the urge to pull her into his arms again. "I want *you*."

"And marriage and a family."

Micah gently pried one of her hands free and held it loosely in his own. "Eventually, sure."

"I can't—the accident—I can't give you kids." Serena wrenched her hand out of his and turned, her shoulders hunched and quaking.

Micah let out a breath as relief washed through him. "Is that all?"

She stiffened. "What do you mean? You didn't see your face when Ruth told you she was expecting. I can't give you that. It will never be us. Do you understand that?"

"There are other ways to have a family."

Serena blinked.

"I love you, Serena. I want a life with you. We can figure out the details as we go along."

"Are you sure?" Tears shimmered in her wide eyes as they filled with hope.

"Of course. There's foster care and adoption, sponsoring orphans. We have options. Maybe we'll just end up being the best aunt and uncle in the world." Micah brushed her cheek with his thumb. "We don't have to know right now. We just have to be willing to figure it out together."

"Really?"

He took the ring, slipped it back on her finger, and breathed a prayer of thanks when she folded herself into his arms. "Really."

"I'm sorry."

He smiled and rested his forehead on hers. "It's okay. Please don't try to shut me out again, okay? Just talk to me."

"I will. I love you, Micah."

Her lips were salty from her tears, but her arms wound tightly around him. He didn't have all the answers about their future. The upcoming time apart still made his heart constrict. But for now, they were both right where they belonged. Together.

Arcadia Valley Romance:
Six authors. Six series. One community.

Welcome to Arcadia Valley, Idaho, where a foodie culture and romance grow hand-in-hand. Join my friends and me as we release a book every month set in Arcadia Valley. You'll enjoy meeting old friends and making new ones as each of the six authors' books intertwine with the previous stories in this Christian romance series. Get started with Romance Grows in Arcadia Valley and follow along at ArcadiaValleyRomance.com to make sure you don't miss any installments!

www.ArcadiaValleyRomance.com

When chiropractor Daniel Quintana needs a summer
nanny for his twins, it only makes sense to hire Tabitha
Moore. Just back from an extended mission trip, she
needs the job. The fact that she was his wife's best friend
shouldn't matter, and neither should the fact that he finds
her attractive. Daniel's not in the market for relationships
because he's just so bad at them.

Tabitha Moore doesn't want to work for Daniel, because
she knows a terrible secret about his daughters. But when
staying with her sister is no longer an option, she feels
like she has no choice. After all, it's just for the
summer...

With the help of Daniel's five-year-old twins, Daniel and
Tabitha start to become more than friends. Growing
vegetables, rescuing a mama cat and her kittens, eating
delicious Mexican food at El Corazon... all of it makes
these two lonely souls crave to create a family long
term... unless Tabitha's secret rips apart everything
they're starting to build.

Chapter One

Tabitha Moore saw the answer on the library board members' faces even before the head librarian, Charlotte MacGregor, opened her mouth.

"I'm so sorry, Tabby," Charlotte said. "Helping to support a bookmobile in Tanzania sounds wonderful, we're all about getting books into people's hands, but we don't have any funds to organize it."

"Maybe you should hit up some of the bigger literacy organizations," another woman—Elise?—suggested.

Tabitha forced a smile at the board members, who were already gathering up their things, obviously eager to get home for dinner. "Thanks so much for hearing me out," she said into a room that wasn't listening. "If anything changes…"

"We'll contact you, of course." Charlotte said. "We really appreciate you coming in. I wish there were more we could do to help, but with our limited budget…" She patted Tabitha's arm on her way out of the meeting room. "I hope you'll be able to get back on your feet another way."

"I'll be fine." After six years of missionary work in Tanzania, first-world problems like not having a job, or her own place to live, didn't bother Tabitha nearly as much as they would've when she'd headed over there.

But her heart broke for the kids who wouldn't get access to books that could enrich their lives.

"How'd it go?" Tabitha's best friend, Veronica Quintana, walked into the now-deserted meeting room and started helping Tabitha bag up her materials.

"It didn't." Tabitha stuffed her laptop into her briefcase, along with a stack of pamphlets. "No budget."

"What are you going to do?" Veronica perched on the table.

Tabitha leaned against the podium where she'd just given her unsuccessful pitch. "Not sure. I'll figure something out."

Her phone buzzed, and when she picked it up, she saw that the lock screen had three messages from her sister. That couldn't be good. She read through them and then, wordlessly, handed the phone to Veronica.

Veronica skimmed the messages. "She's kicking you out? Seriously?"

"The kids want their bedrooms back. I get it. Kind of." When she'd arrived back in Arcadia Valley, Idaho, she'd crashed at her sister's place. Which meant that her sister's two teenagers had to share a room.

"You've been here less than a week, and those bratty teenagers already…" Veronica clapped a hand over her mouth. "I'm sorry. I know you love your nieces, but they can be selfish. And your sister lets them run the home!"

"She does." And, actually, Tabitha wouldn't mind getting out of the small house. She tried to make a joke of the girls' F-bomb funky music, but it bothered her. Even more troubling were their bad attitudes and language toward their mother. "I just don't know where I'm going to live. I need a job before I can afford anything."

"You can stay with me." Veronica offered.

"You're sweet. And you have two exchange students staying with you in a place that's smaller than my sister's. I don't think it'll work, but you're super kind for offering."

"Keep it in mind. I can squeeze you in if need be." Veronica ran her fingers through long, dark hair so similar to Tabitha's that they'd been pegged for sisters many times. "What are you going to do about a job? I've been looking online for you, but I haven't seen anything."

"Me, too, and I've called everyone I know. I'm going through back issues of the paper and checking out bulletin boards and storefronts, but so far…" She sighed. "All the available jobs seem to require a degree, or a union card, or plain old physical strength I don't have. There's a cleaning service that's hiring, but that's a last resort."

"I can ask Javier if he could take you on at El Corazon." Veronica sounded doubtful.

Tabitha laughed. "I'd be *such* a great waitress. People love having their dinners dropped in their laps."

Veronica snickered. "You always were a bit of a klutz."

"I know. And I also know the Lord will provide. I just wish He'd hurry up."

They walked out into the main room of the Arcadia Valley library. Charlotte was back at the front desk, and the place buzzed with students doing homework, senior citizens using the computers, and kids engaged in what sounded like a story time, judging from the rhythmic clapping and happy laughter from the children's room.

Tabitha wanted to linger. She loved libraries, and reading, and children. This was a much more enjoyable environment than her sister's overcrowded home.

Suddenly, Veronica clutched her arm. "You said you hoped God would hurry up?"

"Yeah." Tabitha looked in the direction Veronica was looking. To where a familiar, good-looking man and two identical, sobbing little girls were coming through the door.

"I think the solution to your problem just walked in," Veronica said.

Tabitha's mind raced faster than her heart rate. Was Daniel Quintana a solution, or an even bigger problem?

Daniel Quintana tried to shake off a long day's work so he could deal with the immediate, kids-having-a-tantrum crisis. "Girls," he said firmly, stopping his five-year-old twins just inside the door to Arcadia Valley's library. "Quiet, or we leave."

Kaylee, always obedient, blinked and gulped and managed to stop crying.

Haylee yelled louder.

Daniel sighed. That was the tough thing about raising twins. How did he reward Kaylee for doing what he'd asked, while correcting Haylee for her misbehavior?

"Daniel!" His sister Veronica approached like a rescuing angel. "What's going on?" She knelt in front of Kaylee and gave her a hug, then pulled out a tissue to wipe her face.

"I tried to give them carrots for a snack and they freaked out. They hate vegetables, but it was all that was in the fridge."

Still sobbing dramatically, Haylee reached for her aunt, but Daniel held her by the shoulders. "If you can't stop fussing, we have to leave the library."

Instantly, Haylee's tears evaporated. "Hi, Aunt Veronica," she said in a sunny voice.

"Hi, sweetie. What are you all doing here right at dinnertime?"

Daniel winced at the reminder. "When I got home, the substitute sitter was on her phone and the girls hadn't gone to the library like she promised them."

"Daddy yelled at her," Haylee volunteered.

"Cuz she 'glected us," Kaylee said in her quieter voice.

"Is that so." Veronica gave Daniel a look that clearly said *you're being difficult.*

Heat rose in Daniel's neck. He *was* known for being a bit controlling with his employees in his chiropractic practice, and he shouldn't have yelled, but really, what was he paying the woman for? His house had been trashed, his girls foraging for food in the cupboards, and a random dog—who turned out to be the sitter's— eating from an overturned canister of cereal on the floor.

Meanwhile, the adult in charge was engaged in an off-color telephone fight with her boyfriend.

"Daniel, you remember Tabitha Moore, right?"

The name rang in his ears as his heart picked up its pace and confusion swirled inside his head. He looked up and saw a very grown up, pretty woman in place of the girl who'd been so eager to leave Arcadia Valley six years ago.

"Hi, Daniel," she said, holding out a hand, concern in her dark eyes. "I'm so sorry I couldn't get back for Renee's funeral."

It took him a moment to process what she said. Belatedly, he reached out to shake hands. Hers were rough and callused, at odds with her professional dress and perfect hair. "I know it wasn't possible, with you being so far away. I really appreciated the note you sent."

"That's a pretty necklace," Haylee said. "Can I see?"

Tabitha knelt in front of the girls. "Hi," she said, seeming a little shy herself. She lifted her necklace so they could see it better. "It's from Tanzania. Do you know anything about Africa?"

"People are poor there," Haylee said gravely.

"We saw in Sunday School," Kaylee added.

Tabitha nodded. "A lot of people are poor there, it's true, but not everybody. Some people in Africa are wonderful artists and jewelry makers. A friend of mine made me this necklace, and these earrings, too." She pushed back her hair to show dangling wooden elephants that matched the necklace.

As the girls continued to talk to Tabitha, Daniel blew out a breath. He had no reason to feel guilty, just because he'd socialized with Tabitha a few times in high school. It had all been casual, in a group. Soon after that, he'd started to date her best friend Renee, and the rest had been history.

"This is the perfect solution!" Veronica grabbed Daniel's arm with the certainty of a bossy little sister. "Tabitha's looking for a job, and you're looking for a summer nanny. And you have the mother-in-law suite where she could stay. What could be better?" She reached down and put a hand on Tabitha's shoulder. "Right?"

Tabitha rose gracefully to her feet. "What's that?"

Veronica repeated her proposition while Daniel's mind raced and his stomach churned. As soon as there was a break in Veronica's enthusiastic sales job, he broke in. "Tabitha doesn't want to work as a nanny," he said. "She has a college degree, or most of one. She's looking for a job in the missions field. Aren't you?"

"But she loves kids, and she's been working with them in Tanzania. Literacy and teaching. She loves books."

"We do, too!" Haylee grabbed Tabitha's hand. "Could you be our nanny?"

Tabitha's quick laugh sounded a little forced. "Whoa, let's slow down, everybody." She glanced at Daniel and then down at the girls. "I'm glad for the chance to get to know you girls, and I hope I'll see you this summer. But..." She glanced at Daniel and trailed off.

Good. She didn't want the job any more than he wanted her to have it. Although, uncharacteristically for him, he didn't know why.

"You're looking for a different kind of job, I know," Veronica said. "But you haven't found one yet, and while you look…"

"You're so kind, Veronica," she said. "And I appreciate your trying to help me, I really do. But—"

"I'm hungry," Kaylee said plaintively.

"I'm *starving*!" Haylee tugged at Daniel's hand.

Daniel snapped to attention, looking at the girls. "Let's take back our library books, and pick out one more each, quickly, and then—"

"We'll all meet at El Corazon to talk about Tabitha working as your nanny!" Veronica interrupted.

"Yeah!" Haylee cried. "Let's go see Uncle Javier and eat 'chiladas!'"

"You'll come, won't you?" Veronica asked Tabitha. "It's on us. We're so happy you're back in town. Javier and Molly will want to hear all about your work. They've been following your blog for months."

"I'm a little tired—"

"Come on. I've barely seen you. Please?"

"Can we, Daddy?" Haylee asked.

Daniel blew out a sigh. He ought to get to his family's restaurant more often. He'd grown up there, basically, and he was the only one of the four siblings who wasn't involved.

It was one of the many ways he didn't fit into his family. The restaurant business was too messy and unpredictable for him, the work too loud and social.

But his girls needed the chance to bond with family. Even more so, because they lacked a mother.

"All right," he said. "Let's hurry up and pick out your books, and we'll go over there for a quick dinner." He looked at Tabitha. "Tabitha, it's great to see you again. But please don't feel obligated to take this job Veronica's trying to spring on you."

"Thanks, I..."

"I do need to find a new sitter, or preferably a live-in nanny," he said. "But I'll find somebody. It's not your problem."

"Sure. Thanks. Nice to see you again." She turned and hurried out of the library.

He looked after her. She'd gotten so poised and professional. But he had the odd impression that she didn't want to talk to him.

"I'll make her come to the restaurant, don't worry." Veronica hugged the girls quickly and then hurried after her friend.

And Daniel didn't know whether to hope she succeeded, or hope she didn't.

Because he felt so guilty that occasionally, throughout his difficult marriage, he'd wondered what would have happened if he'd pursued Tabitha instead of Renee.

Tabitha drove her ancient-but-new-to-her subcompact through the streets of Arcadia Valley, trying to delay the confrontation at El Corazon.

What do I do, Father?

Haylee and Kaylee were sweet girls, and Daniel seemed just as she remembered—buttoned down, serious, and hard to read. The care he showed for his daughters didn't surprise her, because he'd always been a champion to those who needed him.

He was also the most handsome of the Quintana brothers, at least to her.

In front of the library, Veronica had continued to push for her to become Haylee and Kaylee's nanny, arguing that this was God's answer to her problems: where to live, how to make a living.

Maybe it was.

Maybe it wasn't, and no way could she tell Veronica why.

She drove down Main Street, noticing the businesses that were new since she'd spent time here. She wanted to check out The Beanery and especially Page Turners—she adored bookstores, small ones in particular. The Sunrise Café was new, but there was the good, old Jukebox, a high school hangout from years past.

She swung around Founders Park, where she and her sister had spent many hours playing. They'd been sent out of the house more often than most kids, what with their parents' problems.

The source of those problems nudged at her, but she firmly pushed it away as she wove through the side streets of Arcadia Valley. She'd come back home to do as Renee had asked, but she was glad to be here. Arcadia Valley was a warm, welcoming town.

Just as long as she didn't probe too deeply into her memories.

She drove past a community garden—that was new—and Benita's gourmet market. Contemplated driving back downtown to check out shoes at Wallman's. But she'd have to face this situation and her choices sometime.

The possibility of working as a nanny for Daniel's girls would certainly allow her to fulfill Renee's commission, sent to her in a letter right before she'd died. She'd been neglecting it for four years, serving in a part of Tanzania where the threat of famine was worsening and the refugee population growing. The mission's work had been gripping, and in some ways she'd hated to leave, but it was time to do as her friend had requested and keep an eye on the girls.

But her best friend had put her in a bind by requesting that she keep a terrible secret.

When Renee had come to Tanzania on a short-term mission trip five years ago, a short while after she'd gotten married, she'd sworn Tabitha to secrecy and then confessed that she'd had an affair.

She'd just learned she was pregnant. And she didn't know who was the father of the twins she was carrying.

Tabitha tried to be a good person and she believed in loyalty to her friends. But she also believed in telling the truth. And if she worked for Daniel, as a nanny for his twins, she couldn't escape the reality that would face her every day: those two little girls who obviously doted on their father might not even be his.

Books in the Arcadia Valley Romance Series

Want a Free Book?

If you enjoyed Muffins & Moonbeams and would like to read one of my full-length novels for free, you can get a free download of Courage to Change simply by signing up for my newsletter here: http://bit.ly/2g0AGvf

Author's Note

Thank you for reading Cookies & Candlelight! I hope that you enjoyed it! I would appreciate it if you'd help others enjoy it too by leaving a review! Word of mouth is how most people say they find new books to read, so I'd love it if you'd also consider telling your friends about it. Any success my books have is owed to readers like you who take the time to tell others about my stories. Thank you, from the bottom of my heart.

Working on this project, with the five other amazing authors who are all writing in Arcadia Valley, has been an absolute delight. I love all the characters who fill up our little town, and I hope you will, too. Each of the ladies who are a part of Arcadia Valley has a great talent and a deep love for Christian fiction. I think you'll agree it shows in the work they produce.

You can always keep up to date with my writing news via my newsletter. There's a sign-up form at my website http://bit.ly/2g0AGvf and also on my author Facebook page

http://www.Facebook.com/ElizabethMaddrey.

I continue to owe a huge debt of gratitude to my husband and sons for giving me the time to write, my sister for her unflinching support and encouragement, and my critique partners Valerie Comer, Lynellen Perry, Heather Gray and Jan Elder for catching all the times I use the same word six times in two paragraphs.

More than anything, I'm grateful that God continues to give me words and makes it possible for me to write them down.

I'd love to hear from you! You can connect with me on Facebook my webpage or via email.

About the Author

Elizabeth Maddrey began writing stories as soon as she could form the letters properly and has never looked back. Though her practical nature and love of computers, math, and organization steered her into computer science at Wheaton College, she always had one or more stories in progress to occupy her free time. This continued through a Master's program in Software Engineering, several years in the computer industry, teaching programming at the college level, and a Ph.D. in Computer Technology in Education. When she isn't writing, Elizabeth is a voracious consumer of books and has mastered the art of reading while undertaking just about any other activity.

Elizabeth is the author of more than ten books, both fiction and non-fiction. She lives in the suburbs of Washington, D.C. with her husband and their two incredibly active little boys.

www.ingramcontent.com/pod-product-compliance
Lightning Source LLC
Chambersburg PA
CBHW030247200626
46816CB00002BA/541